Title

On-

Format: Jacketed Hardcover

ISBN: 978-1-338-78984-3 || Price: $18.99 US

Ages: 8–12

Grades: 3–7

LOC Number: Available

Length: 256 pages

Trim: 5-1/2 x 8-1/4 inches

Classification:
Juvenile Fiction / Action & Adventure / Survival Stories
Juvenile Fiction / Legends, Myths, Fables / Asian
Juvenile Fiction / Diversity & Multicultural

---------------- *Additional Formats Available* --------------
Ebook ISBN: 978-1-338-78985-0
Digital Audiobook ISBN: 978-1-5461-2092-6 || Price: $27.99 US
Library Audiobook ISBN: 978-1-5461-2093-3 || Price: $83.99 US

Scholastic Press
An Imprint of Scholastic Inc.
557 Broadway, New York, NY 10012
For information, contact us at:
tradepublicity@scholastic.com

THE CROSSBOW OF DESTINY

THE CROSSBOW OF DESTINY

BRANDON HOÀNG

SCHOLASTIC PRESS • NEW YORK

Library of Congress Cataloging-in-Publication Data available

ISBN 978-1-338-78984-3

10 9 8 7 6 5 4 3 2 1   24 25 26 27 28

Printed in U.S.A.   66
First edition, August 2024

Book design by Christopher Stengel

To my cousin Amy Quyên and
to all Viet cousins everywhere.
No one shows up for you like a Viet cousin.

[Map of Vietnam, TK]

Long ago in the ancient country of Âu Lạc.

Before Vietnam was Vietnam . . .

Cao Lỗ's hands were shaking. He massaged his twitching fingers, then rubbed his tired eyes. There was no time for rest: General Zhao Tuo and his massive army would be at the citadel at any moment—and they meant to take it this time.

The gifted engineer shifted the crossbow to his shoulder, testing its weight. It had some heft to it; not too heavy, but not too light either. King An Dương had given his childhood friend and trusted weaponry architect permission to use whatever resources he needed to construct this unique crossbow. The wood was cut from the hidden glade where Cao Lỗ and the king romped as children, and the weapon's trigger and buttplate were made of exquisite bronze inlaid with deep green jade.

It was Cao Lỗ's masterpiece.

A knock at the door jolted the engineer from his trance.

"Come in," said Cao Lỗ, brushing his thumb over the crossbow's intricate engravings.

King An Dương stepped inside the chambers. He looked almost as weary as Cao Lỗ. "I don't mean to rush you, my friend, but General Zhao Tuo and his men approach."

The engineer raised a finger. "I need to fit the last piece."

The king locked the door behind him, put his ear to the door, and when he was satisfied they were alone, he extended his hand to the engineer. In the king's palm lay a turtle's claw.

So it was real.

Cao Lỗ plucked the claw from the king's hand. It didn't feel divine or magical. The king claimed the claw had come to him in a dream. He had prayed, ordered that incense sticks be burned around the clock, anything to earn the gods' favor to help fend off General Zhao Tuo's attacks. And it worked: One night, a golden turtle appeared at the foot of the king's bed and instructed him to build a custom crossbow that would fit the claw.

"Whoever wields the crossbow rules the realm," declared the turtle-god. "Whoever wields the crossbow... controls destiny. This weapon will give you what you desire, but be warned: When you have succeeded in defending your kingdom, you must return the claw to me—or you will pay with your blood."

And when the king awoke, he found the turtle's claw on his pillow.

Cao Lỗ slid the claw where a traditional crossbow's tumbler was supposed to be. A perfect fit. The engineer smiled. He could still surprise himself with his own creations.

"And you're sure this will work? This turtle-god can be trusted?" Cao Lỗ asked, handing over the crossbow. The gods could sometimes be mischievous, meddling with humans and their affairs as if they were game pieces.

"A risk we must take. If not, we are doomed." The king inspected the crossbow, carefully turning it in his hands. A glint shimmered in his eye. "You've outdone yourself this time, old friend. When I fire the first arrow, I'd like nothing more than to have you by my side."

"But what if the crossbow fails?" Cao Lỗ asked.

The king grinned. "Then we will die together."

Cao Lỗ bowed, accepting the invitation. Even after all this time, he felt silly displaying such formality to his dearest childhood friend.

As they approached the top of the city's outer walls, Cao Lỗ shuddered at the massive sight before him. General Zhao Tuo's army had arrived. Hundreds upon hundreds of soldiers stood in perfect formation, their spears glistening, war banners unfurled. Their horses pawed the ground, eyes hungry for battle.

General Zhao Tuo rode to the front of the line, his son Trọng Thủy flanking him.

"King An Dươngof Âu Lạc!" shouted the general. "I call on your formal surrender."

Cao Lỗ snuck a glance at his friend—no, at the king. There was an iciness to King An Dương's stare, enough to send a shiver down the engineer's back.

"And in return, I offer you a chance to save your men," said King An Dương, his voice cool and steady. "Leave my kingdom, return home, and you'll be spared."

"You can't win," General Zhao Tuo said, smirking

as his son fought to keep a brave face. "Who will save you now?"

King An Dương raised the crossbow. "The gods."

Cao Lỗ jolted awake. The engineer was exhausted, but whenever he shut his eyes, the visions of what happened at the gates of Âu Lạc tormented him. In the weeks that followed, the general from the north refused to admit defeat. Every time, General Zhao Tuo and his son fled from the battlefield, only to return with more men. And every time, King An Dương drove them back with his divine weapon. The screams and howls from the fallen soldiers rang in Cao Lỗ's ears. Some soldiers pleaded to the gods for relief. All of them begged for their mothers. The ending was always the same: When the golden arrows flew from the magic crossbow, the general's armies melted like snow falling on warm ground.

But that victory came at a price. When King An Dương fired the crossbow, it was as if he paid with a piece of his soul. There were nights the king wandered the hallways, muttering to himself. The king wasn't sleeping. The king wasn't eating. Most days he'd hide away in the armory where he kept the crossbow and simply hold it in his lap for hours. King An Dương was deteriorating. Cao Lỗ wondered if he made a mistake by agreeing to build that cursed weapon.

Eventually, General Zhao Tuo was forced to admit that Âu Lạc was impenetrable, and he called King An Dương for a truce. As a sign of peace, General Zhao Tuo sent Trọng Thủy to offer his hand in marriage to King An Dương's daughter, Princess Mị Châu. When Cao Lỗ caught word of this, he felt a deep pit of worry grow in his gut; he wasn't so sure the general could be trusted. But whenever Cao Lỗ tried to raise his concern to King An Dương, the king waved him off. It wasn't like the king to be so dismissive of his most trusted friend and advisor, but ever since he first fired the crossbow, the king hadn't acted like himself. He'd become irritable, snapping without provocation.

"Do you want peace?" King An Dương growled.

"Yes, of course," replied Cao Lỗ, careful to temper his voice.

"You disapprove of the gift the gods have bestowed upon me. I can see it in your eyes," said the king. Cao Lỗ knew better than to speak. "So, the way I see it, the only way to peace is by accepting my enemy's offer—to have his son join us. Or would you rather I take up the crossbow once more?"

Cao Lỗ bowed. It seemed like all he did these days was bow.

It wasn't until Trọng Thủy married Princess Mị Châu that King An Dương's mood finally shifted. It was the happiest Cao Lỗ had seen his friend in months. Joining the families through marriage would bring prosperity and peace to the kingdom. And while Cao Lỗ was delighted to see King An Dương in good spirits, he knew that harmony in Âu Lạc would not last.

Cao Lỗ waited for the perfect opportunity to talk to King An Dương about the turtle's claw. That moment would come when Princess Mị Châu gave birth to a baby boy and Âu Lạc rejoiced. After the celebration died down, Cao Lỗ approached his friend and once again tried to convince him to return the claw to the golden turtle. He found King An Dương in the armory admiring the claw. The moonlight seemed to glisten off it.

But the king was not pleased at Cao Lỗ's suggestion.

"I grow tired of you questioning me at every turn," snarled King An Dương. "And now you question me again on the day my grandson is born. You've forgotten your place."

This time, Cao Lỗ refused to bow. "You haven't been yourself since the first arrow flew. The crossbow consumes you. It must be returned."

"Would you not have me use this gift to save our people?"

"You have succeeded," Cao Lỗ fired back. "It is time to return the claw where it belongs, as the god instructed."

"Why stop at peace?" King An Dương volleyed, eyeing the claw as if it called his name. "With the crossbow by my side, I can ensure Âu Lạc's prosperity for all time—perhaps even expand it."

"Then you are no better than the general!" The words flew out of Cao Lỗ's mouth before he could stop them.

King An Dương seemed to be just as shocked by the engineer's outburst, for he did not speak. Cao Lỗ seized the opportunity.

"I don't know what the gods intended," he continued, "but I cannot believe any deity that is benevolent and merciful would have us inflict this kind of pain to another living creature, especially with a divine weapon. You may be a king, but you are no god."

"Then you are a traitor to me and a traitor to your kingdom!"

The king wheeled around, aiming the crossbow at Cao Lỗ's heart.

Cao Lỗ did not cower; he did not flinch. But a tear rolled down his cheek.

His friend was gone.

King An Dương's finger twitched over the crossbow's trigger. The two men regarded each other with something akin to confusion, anger, and sadness, as if they had just wandered into a land from which they could never return.

"I should kill you where you stand for speaking to me in such a manner," said the king at last, lowering the weapon. "However, I will spare your life because you are— you *were*—once a friend to me. But if I see you again, you will know the crossbow's power firsthand. Be gone."

Cao Lỗ packed what little possessions he owned—his tools, a waterskin, some feed for his horse—but before he left the kingdom of Âu Lạc, Cao Lỗ sought out the princess.

"You know your father isn't himself. You must take the crossbow from him," Cao Lỗ begged.

"But how?" asked Princess Mị Châu. "You know as

well as I do that my father doesn't let the crossbow out of his sight."

"With this." Cao Lỗ slipped his hand in his robes and pulled out an exact replica of the turtle's claw that he had created. "You are the only one he trusts to get close. Swap out the claw with this fake tumbler. Without the claw, the crossbow is nothing."

The engineer placed the claw in Princess Mị Châu's open palm and closed her fingers around it. He did not wait for an answer.

Cao Lỗ left the kingdom but secretly kept eyes on the princess. He learned through his spies that Princess Mị Châu enlisted the help of Trọng Thủy—now *Prince Trọng Thủy*—to make the exchange, and they succeeded. What Cao Lỗ didn't know was that the prince would return home to inform General Zhao Tuo of what had transpired.

Âu Lạc was vulnerable once more. Armed with this new knowledge, General Zhao Tuo did not hesitate. He sent down his great army for the last time. King An Dương took to the outer wall, prepared as always to defend his kingdom. But this time, when the king released the crossbow's string, golden arrows did not fill the night sky—only the cries of war as General Zhao Tuo's soldiers breached the city gates, swarming like angry ants.

Âu Lạc fell within a matter of hours.

King An Dương mounted his horse and fled, the crossbow sheathed on the horse's saddle. Princess Mị Châu rode on the back, trying to quiet the wailing baby in her arms. They rode for days through dense jungles, crisscrossing mountains, seeking refuge in neighboring provinces, and traversing unknown lands occupied by unknown kingdoms. Finally, when the king and his daughter reached the sea, King An Dương pulled hard on the reins and the horse skidded to a halt. There was nowhere left to go.

King An Dương clasped his hands in prayer and tears streaked down his face. Behind him, Princess Mị Châu sobbed.

"Why have you forsaken me?" asked King An Dương. "Why have you taken away my power?"

And then a golden shell crested the waves.

"It was never your power," the golden turtle addressed the king. "It was mine. It has always been mine. And I have come to claim it."

King An Dương offered up the crossbow without a second thought.

The turtle slowly shook his craggy head. "That is not my claw."

"W-what do you m-mean?" the king asked, his voice trembling with fear.

The turtle's eyes glanced past the king's shoulder. "Ask the one behind you where it is."

King An Dương turned to meet his daughter's gaze, his eyes wide with realization.

Princess Mị Châu threw herself from the horse, cradling the baby, and dropped to her knees. She tugged at her father's robes and begged for mercy.

But there was no mercy, no hesitation: King An Dương drew his sword and struck down his daughter. It was quick. She felt no pain.

Then came the thundering of hooves. Prince Trọng Thủy had arrived.

"How did you find us?" The king spat, drawing his sword once more.

Prince Trọng Thủy didn't answer. Instead he drew his own sword. "What have you done?"

They clashed. The king fought for vengeance. The prince fought for his family. By the time Cao Lỗ reached the beach, it was too late. Both were evenly matched. Prince Trọng Thủy was dead and King An Dương was left mortally wounded.

Cao Lỗ found the turtle claw in Prince Trọng Thủy's

clenched fist, and he took it. The engineer kneeled before King An Dương and shoved the claw into his shaky hand. "Return it. Do it now. The claw must be returned by your hands."

King An Dương grinned, bearing his blood-stained teeth. He stared at the sea, then back to his old friend.

"No," he breathed.

Cao Lỗ placed the turtle claw back onto the crossbow. A satisfying click rang out as the claw snapped into place, and the crossbow radiated a golden glow. Cao Lỗ could feel the warm power ripple through his body—a power that was absolute.

It was the sound of a baby's cry that snapped Cao Lỗ out of his stupor. The little prince was still alive.

With the crossbow tucked under one arm and the baby in the other, Cao Lỗ surveyed the death that choked the beach.

The prince.

The princess.

A baby without his father or his mother.

"Look at all this death. All this destruction. And for what?" Cao Lỗ lamented. "They shall never be together again."

2,000 years later . . .
Give or take.

CHAPTER 1

"Freddie, you're missing it!"

Freddie blinked herself awake, wiping the corner of her mouth, slightly embarrassed that she'd drooled in her sleep. The week leading up to the trip to Vietnam, Freddie tried preparing herself for the inevitable jetlag by staying up until odd hours. Apparently, her training didn't work. The gentle, rhythmic clickety-clack of the train tracks didn't exactly help keep her awake either.

"Sometimes I worry about you," said Freddie's mom, Diễm, nudging her. "I swear if I wasn't here, you'd never wake up for anything."

"What can I say? I'm a growing girl." Freddie checked

to make sure she didn't get any drool on her cousin Liên's regulation-size Home Depot box. Liên specifically instructed Freddie to triple duct-tape it for extra security and sent her no fewer than four follow-up emails to make sure.

Mom put an arm around Freddie and planted a kiss on her daughter's forehead. "What do you think? Do you recognize any of it?"

Freddie gazed out the window. The train glided alongside perfectly symmetrical squares of rice fields, sun beams gleaming off their muddied waters. Floppy-eared goats were free to wander on the side of the road, lazily hunting for patches of grass. A fleet of fishing boats bobbed in the sea. And beyond that was the mountain range from which her sleepy seaside town got its name—a small rock poking from the water like a turtle's head, followed by a jagged cliff that created what looked like a turtle's shell.

Vỏ Rùa Làng. Turtle Shell Village.

They passed houses with paint-chipped window shutters that had signs promising food like the spicy beef noodle soup bún bò Huế, or the refreshing tomato-infused fish broth made with jellyfish, bún cá sứa. Freddie used to pick around the gelatinous pieces of jellyfish—that, she could remember. She wondered how any of these homes managed to get any business; there was no foot traffic and the homes seemed so isolated in their pockets nestled in the quiet countryside.

As to whether she remembered this seaside route, it was hard to say. There was a feeling, deep in her gut, that told Freddie she was back home. But these feelings were blips that fizzled out as quickly as they came, her memories more like echoes whose source she couldn't quite place. Being back in Vietnam after all this time felt like the first few moments after being woken up from a deep sleep, trying to collect her thoughts and orient herself.

"Sort of" was the best answer she could muster, and even that came out more of a grumble.

"Hey, hey, Mặt Xấu." Mom tugged Freddie's chin toward her so she could look into Freddie's light brass-brown eyes.

Ugly Face? Freddie translated in her head, then sulked.

"What's with the frown? Let's check our attitude. You can't bring your usual brand of sass to this side of your family. Not on this trip."

"I don't know why we had to come back *this*

summer." Freddie rolled her eyes. "Nisa and Tash and I had the whole summer totally mapped out."

Mom sighed. She was sighing more and more these days. "I think you could spend less time with Nisa and Tash covering our tax-funded sidewalk curbs with your skateboard wax and more time hitting that summer reading list."

Freddie shook her head, tucked her knee under her chin, and went back to looking out the window.

"I'm serious, Freddie. I know things are a little . . . weird right now with your dad and me, but high school will be here before you know it, and that's the real deal. Might as well lay the foundation now." Mom reached to push a strand of dark hair behind Freddie's ear. "You're Vietnamese. You have it in you to push past whatever this is. You have to endure, my girl."

Freddie pushed Mom's hand away and mumbled something.

"What was that?" asked Mom.

"Half," said Freddie. "I'm only *half* Viet."

Now it was Mom's turn to frown. She started to say something but checked her watch instead. "We should be there soon."

Freddie took a deep breath, wrapped up her earbuds,

and clasped her video game shut. She pulled out her manga from the front seat pocket and read the same page twice before giving up.

The train squealed into the station. There wasn't much to it—a sagging roof and a small lemon-yellow building whose paint was peeling. A lone vending machine hummed next to the tiny ticket window. Mom reminded Freddie to triple check that she had her bags and Liên's package, then made a special point to see Freddie hold out her dark blue passport.

Be very careful not to lose your passport, Freddie recalled her mother warning for the twentieth time before they left Oregon. *You can't get home without it!*

Once Mom was satisfied, Freddie shouldered her backpack and lugged her suitcase down the aisle.

A blast of warm air hit Freddie as she stepped off the train. She tugged on her button down shirt, peeling the damp fabric away from her sweaty back. The humidity, the heat—it was all coming back to her. But she wasn't annoyed by the stifling air; it felt familiar in a cozy sort of way, almost like a warm hug.

Which was more than Freddie could say about her

mom, who hadn't waited for Freddie. She was clearly still annoyed at her daughter. Not that Freddie could blame her. Freddie hadn't exactly made life easy for anyone since Dad moved out, and it seemed she was about to do the same to this trip too.

Freddie felt a twinge of guilt. "Mom, I'm sorr—"

But the apology never left her lips because something caught her eye. Standing next to the vending machine was a somewhat lankygirl nervously tugging at a seafoam-green sundress, a matching hat with a bow, and a pair of chunky white sandals. Her black hair was cut in a neat bob down to her chin. The lenses of her enormous spectacles, which were at least a size too big for her round face, gleamed in the afternoon sun. When her eyes connected with Freddie's, she made a slight bow with her head.

"Liên!" Freddie beamed and raced toward the girl, dropping the box. She threw her arms around Liên, knocking her hat to the ground. "Don't hide that little head bow! Get outta here with the formalities!"

Liên chuckled, pushing her frames up the bridge of her clover-shaped nose. She'd worn glasses ever since she was a toddler, and for as long as Freddie could remember, Liên's glasses were always sliding down.

21

"I don't know!" she said in perfect English. "We haven't seen each other in person since we were little!" Somehow Liên managed to make her own form of English dialect cute, like a smooth, clean, meandering stream with only the faintest wisp of an accent. Unlike Freddie's clunky Vietnamese.

"We FaceTime like every month! You *know* me!" Freddie stepped back to get a better look. "I can't believe it. You really cut your hair! It looks great."

"You think so? I'm trying something new. My mom thinks I committed some kind of crime by cutting it all off." Blushing, Liên smoothed her hair before pickingup her sunhat. "So . . . how does it feel to be back?"

Freddie put her hands on her hips, taking in the train station. "I'm not sure yet."

"Well, maybe it'll feel different when you see the house." Liên opened a coin purse shaped like a cute kitten head and peeled out a colorful bill. "You thirsty?"

Freddie nodded, not realizing how parched she was. She hadn't had anything to drink since Saigon.

Liên inserted the bill into the vending machine, made a selection, and then handed Freddie a bottle with a yellow label. Freddie could only make out the word *Lemona*. Probably something that tasted of lemons was the best she could deduce. The rest of the bottle's label was a total mystery as she'd never learned how to read Vietnamese. By the time she'd left the country when she was five, she was only just learning to.

"It's just mineral water," said Liên, sensing Freddie's hesitation. "With like a lemon twist, if that makes sense."

Freddie felt a twinge of embarrassment. "Yeah, I knew that," she said, quickly shrugging it off as she unscrewed the cap and guzzled the bubbly water.

Thankfully, Liên's attention was redirected to the box at Freddie's feet. "You brought it!"

"Of course," said Freddie, happy to skirt the fact that she couldn't read Vietnamese. "I mean, it was kind of a pain in the butt to lug around, but what are cousins for?"

Liên started after the box but stopped herself, looking at Freddie for permission.

Freddie laughed. "Go nuts. It's *your* stuff."

Liên tore into the box, pulling out items and ogling them as if she was excavating an ancient tomb. "Spicy Sweet Chili Doritos! Real Ranch dressing! Oh, and you even got good shampoo! Were you able to get any of those Sour Patch Kids?"

"Oh, uh . . ." Freddie had thrown together the items at the last minute, and that was only after her mom had harassed her about it three or four times. She may have forgotten some stuff on Liên's wish list. "Sorry, the place I went to was fresh out."

"Don't worry about it," said Liên with a shrug. "I would have been happy with anything you brought over. I'm telling you, you can't get this stuff here. Cảm ơn! Thank you!"

"I'll leave you alone with your bounty," said Freddie. "If you see my mom, tell her I'm going to the bathroom."

"Oh! Dì Diễm!" Liên blushed, covering her mouth with her hands. "I didn't even say hello! What kind of niece am I?" She grabbed the box, Freddie's luggage, and rushed off. "We're parked out back when you're finished."

Freddie had no trouble finding the bathroom because all the signs had pictures on them. She finished up and headed to the parking lot to find Mom and Liên. But when she turned a corner, she slammed right into someone, causing her to stumble and drop her backpack, its contents spilling out.

"Hey! Watch it!" said Freddie, hurriedly collecting as much of her belongings as she could. Then she looked up and froze, startled.

She saw the face of a stern station agent. He wore a permanent scowl on his face, his eyebrows bushy and wild. His thick neck bulged under a crisp, baby blue collared shirt. Yellow epaulets were planted on each of his broad shoulders and an official-looking blue cap was tucked under a muscled arm. A large knife was sheathed at his hip. The station agent made a few sharp tugs to his uniform as he growled something in Vietnamese. Whatever he said, his tone was dry, almost accusatory.

Freddie started to speak, but she couldn't find the words. Eventually she managed to choke out, "My Vietnamese is a little rusty . . ."

His expression softened but only slightly. He bent down and picked up her passport.

Freddie felt her cheeks flush again. "Sorry—uh, xin lỗi. I didn't know I—"

"Hãy cẩn thận . . . Freddie," said the station agent.

Freddie struggled to translate. *Be more careful?* There was something strange about his tone. It wasn't friendly advice. It felt more like . . . a warning. Before Freddie could process the situation further, the station agent had already turned on his heel and disappeared out a side exit.

Freddie stood, finally allowing herself to shiver before checking the passport. She opened it, turned it over. Everything looked fine. Freddie should have been relieved, but all she felt was a cold shiver down her spine.

How did this stranger know her name?

CHAPTER 2

Freddie's family was waiting for her in the parking lot behind the train station. They were standing around a gray minivan trying to fit the last bit of luggage into the trunk as if it were a game of Tetris. Freddie recognized everyone from pictures and the sporadic birthday, Christmas, and Lunar New Year video calls. The whole family was there—well, everyone except the one person she was most looking forward to seeing: her ông ngoại, her grandfather. Freddie's heart sank. Didn't he want to greet her at the station?

Uncle Thanh, the eldest sibling in the Lỗ family, was the first to spot Freddie. The wet toothpick dangling from his lips nearly fell to the ground when their eyes met. He wore a Tiger Beer T-shirt rolled up to his chest like a makeshift crop-top, providing a fresh breeze while exposing his belly. He gave Freddie's suitcase a sharp nudge with his hip and closed the van's trunk.

"What did you pack in here, the Statue of Liberty?" He blinked fast, laughing at his own joke.

"Hi, Bác Thanh," Freddie said as she went in for a hug.

Her uncle clasped his hands in prayer and bowed. "Welcome back, Công chúa Măng cụt." Bác Thanh laughed again, the wrinkles around his eyes crinkling.

Freddie struggled to get the joke.

"He's joking, Freddie." Mom poked her head out of the window of the front passenger seat. "Do you remember Công chúa Măng cụt?"

"Công chúa . . . Măng cụt?" Freddie repeated. Was it some kind of slang that she'd forgotten? "Princess . . . Mangosteen?"

"That's right!" said Bác Thanh, ruffling Freddie's hair. "If we didn't keep a close eye on you, you'd steal all the mangosteen and wouldn't share them with anyone else. You ate so many that we thought you'd turn purple. So we called you Công chúa Măng cụt! But I guess now we should be calling you . . . Miss America!"

Freddie climbed into the van. "Oh, yeah, that definitely sounds like something I'd do . . ."

It wasn't lost on her that everyone slipped in and out of Vietnamese and randomly switched to English when addressing her. Sometimes Freddie found herself responding in choppy Vietnamese. Mostly in English. There was no reason or consistency. On their last call together, Liên had assured Freddie that her Vietnamese would only get stronger the more time she spent back in the country. Like riding a bike. Except Freddie's bike was covered in cobwebs, squeaky with rust, missing a couple gears, and the chain dragged on the gravel.

Freddie's Aunt Hoa and Uncle Lộc, Liên's parents, sat in the center seats. Liên inherited her mom's fashion sense. Both always looked so fancy without a hair out of place, but they made it look so natural and easy. Liên's stick-out ears were definitely a product of her dad.

"Hi, Bác Hoa! Hi, Bác Lộc!" Freddie gave half-hugs as she squeezed her way to Liên at the back of the van. Bác Lộc patted Freddie's shoulder in a jovial way that all Viet uncles do.

"Hi, Con—you hungry?" Bác Hoa pulled Freddie toward her and gave Freddie's cheek a sharp sniff—a sort of classic Vietnamese kiss. "My sister feeding you enough?"

Mom whipped around from the front seat, shooting her sister a playful glare. "What's that supposed to mean?"

"I'm talking about real food! *Vietnamese* food. The food she grew up on!" Bác Hoa said, pounding her fist in her palm. "How's school, Freddie? All As?"

Freddie half expected her mom to stick her tongue out at her. Instead, Mom simply nodded, letting Freddie sweat it out on her own.

"Uh . . ." Freddie blanched. She knew Liên's parents were sticklers about grades. Which Vietnamese parents weren't? Well, except Freddie's mom. "Throw some Bs in there." She lowered her voice to whisper. "And maybe a C . . ."

"See? This is what I'm talking about." Bác Hoa shook her head. "It's that food you eat over there. Full of chemicals. I read that American hot dogs can actually stunt your growth if you eat too much of them. If you were eating my cooking, your brain would get bigger. Look at Liên. All she eats is our family noodles and she's top of her class. Isn't that right, Liên?"

"Mẹ," Liên said, a hint of whine in her voice. "It's

always about my grades? I do other stuff, you know."

"Do you see how she talks to me?" Bác Hoa said, shaking her head. "Ever since I let her cut her hair, she thinks she's an adult who can speak to me like that."

Liên sighed then turned to look out the window. Freddie made a point not to compliment Liên's grades—apparently that was off limits.

"Speaking of food, let's go eat. I'm starved." Bác Hoa leaned forward and tapped Bác Thanh's headrest. "How about the bánh mì place with that nice dog?"

"The big black puppy with the brown patch over her eye?" Mom clapped her hands. "I loved her! She's still around?"

"Not a puppy anymore," said Bác Thanh, dismissing his sister with a wave of his hand. "But I don't want bánh mì, I had it this morning. Let's take the girls for chè."

"Chè?" Bác Hoa playfully slapped the headrest again. "We can't feed them dessert for lunch!"

"You're too strict," Bác Thanh retorted. "Let these kids live a little. Life is too short."

"Life is short because all you eat is dessert!" Mom interjected. "Oh! How about we try that place . . ."

The siblings slipped into their old banter—at least,

it felt that way to Freddie. Even though this was the first time in forever that she was in the same space as her aunt and uncles, Freddie could tell they were closer than close. Even Mom seemed to slide back into the family like an old, comfortable T-shirt. For a moment, Freddie couldn't help but feel jealous; she wished she had that kind of relationship with her aunt and uncles. It made her even more grateful to have Lien by her side, who was practically her sister.

But Freddie couldn't think about that right now. Her mind had drifted back to the station agent.

Freddie looked over her shoulder at Liên. "Something really weird happened back in the bathroom."

Liên's nose wrinkled as she cleaned her glasses with a handkerchief from her purse. "That's between you and your doctor."

Freddie punched Liên in the arm. "I'm being serious. Some creepy uniformed dude came up to me and knocked all my stuff out of my backpack, and then he gave me my passport—"

"So . . . an accident-prone station agent returned your passport?" Liên interrupted. "I'm not seeing the problem."

"And then he called me Freddie!"

Liên stared at Freddie for a moment, waiting for more. "He . . . called you by your name?"

"Well, yeah, but . . . *how* did he know my name, Liên?"

"He must have read your name in your passport when he picked it up." Liên offered a sympathetic shrug.

"Did I mention he had a knife? What kind of station agent carries a knife?" Freddie huffed. She didn't remember the agent actually opening up her passport. But maybe Liên was right. Maybe Freddie's brain was really scrambled from all the traveling. Maybe all Freddie needed was to get another nap in.

"What happened with Ông Ngoại?" asked Freddie, quickly changing the subject. "I kinda hoped he'd be here."

"Ah, well . . . he was going to . . ."

"But?"

"He got pulled into another meeting with his business partner, Nhất."

"Nhất?" The name didn't ring a bell.

"He's been around forever, but I think he met Ông Ngoại after you left," said Liên. "Nhất is the one who's hosting Ông Ngoại's lifetime achievement ceremony, and the one who's been funding Ông Ngoại's research all these years. He's another history buff. Super rich."

Freddie felt a twinge of sadness. If Nhất was this important to Ông Ngoại's life, how come she didn't know about him? It was just another reminder of how much she missed out on being away for so long.

CHAPTER 3

Vỏ Rùa Làng was a humble little town built right next to the seaside, where the Lỗs had lived for generations. It had all the charm of a fishing village with bridges and boats dotting the water, but with a splash of city bustle. The smell of the sea air was the jolt Freddie needed to jog her memory. She suddenly had glimpses of goofing with Liên on the sun-soaked beaches, exploring the nearby markets with her mom, splashing about in the warm ocean water, and harassing the bánh mì vendors for free sandwiches.

Now all Freddie needed was for her Vietnamese to come flooding back.

As they entered the crowded roundabout that led

into town, a sense of wonder washed over Freddie. It felt as if the van were the only four-wheeled vehicle on the road. The streets—which had no painted markings for lanes as far as Freddie could tell—were packed with motorcycles, mopeds, and scooters zipping about from every angle. Tarp tents had been erected and lit with string lights as black-haired, brown-skinned customers in breezy dresses and tank tops and shorts sat in plastic chairs, noshing on skewered meats. They drove past a small graveyard, so small it was easy to miss, with knee-high gravestones adorned with same uniform red writing and overgrown with weeds. A bony stray mutt sleepily watched as beachgoers rinsed the sand off thanks to an outdoor shower structure made from only a few pipes and corrugated metal panels. The town seemed to have its own flow. The motorbikes that whizzed by weaved in and out at their own pace. Even the people wandering the streets had a briskness in their step, and yet there was a casual breeziness to their stroll.

Vỏ Rùa Làng was a little bit of this, a little bit of that.

A little bit like Freddie.

The group never came to an agreement about where to eat; their colorful debate continued even after they arrived at the house. It was easier just to eat at home. One by one, they spilled out of the van, followed by Freddie and Liên.

Freddie couldn't help but stare at her childhood home in awe, taking in every detail. The Lỗ's tall, skinny three-story house was tucked down an alley that was far enough from the noises of the main street, but not so far that they couldn't attract customers. The bright turquoise and bumblebee-yellow paint had faded over the years. The first floor doubled as a kitchen and restaurant, which was known for its bún chả cá—a fried fish cake noodle soup made from a light, almost clear, orange broth and packed with fresh, crunchy veggies. No matter what time of day it was, there was always a pot of broth boiling and someone always had a bowl of steaming noodles in their hands. The second and third floors were where the family lived. The balconies' shuddered doors faced the alley guarded by white wooden rails where potted plants hung, their long vines drooping like tentacles.

Out back was a courtyard that functioned more like a storage unit. Old restaurant equipment that Bác Thanh swore he'd fix or sell someday sat collecting dust. Ladders with missing rungs, rolled-up tarps, dusty beach umbrellas riddled with rips and tears, and broken fans were stacked in some kind of organized chaos. And in the center of it all was a lone mangosteen tree.

Before Freddie could explore, she saw two figures emerge from the front door—a man and a boy who looked about her age. Behind them, with his hands characteristically folded behind his back, was her ông ngoại. His white hair was wild and uncompromising, much like Freddie's. He wore the same uniform as always, a white collared short-sleeved button-down with breezy slacks and sandals. A pair of glasses with chunky black frames and lenses as thick as Liên's balanced on the end of his nose.

"Ah, there you are!" the mysterious man exclaimed, stretching his arms wide in welcome as he approached the van. Despite the heat, he wore a perfectly tailored beige suit. His crisp white dress shirt was cuffed to his elbows, and he slung a jacket over his shoulder. The man's short black hair was meticulously styled, and his bright smile complemented the beaming afternoon sun.

The boy next to the man shared many of his handsome features. Wild strands of hair that hadn't fallen around his face were pulled back in a ponytail, the sides closely shaved underneath. His eyes were the color of a toasted marshmallow with a faint gold rim. His eyebrows were thick and narrowed, giving the impression of a frown. The boy had a stiff, muscled posture that dripped power, like he had a growth spurt that hadn't quite ended. Freddie would have gambled the few dollars she had in her wallet that he was the man's son.

"Trời ơi! Hello!" said the man, turning back to look at Freddie's ông ngoại. "Can this be? Is this really her? Is this the American granddaughter you've been going on about?"

Ông Ngoại's warm brown eyes met Freddie's and he smiled. "The one and only."

The man's smile matched Ông Ngoại's as he gently clasped Freddie's hand in a handshake. He said something to her in Vietnamese and Freddie's ears turned hot. He spoke too quickly with too many unfamiliar words, and she couldn't translate fast enough. This scenario was exactly what she'd been dreading since the plane touched ground.

"Xin lỗi," Freddie mumbled, searching for the words to convey that she didn't understand him. "Tôi không . . . hiểu." Her only way out of this vortex of humiliation was if the man could understand her through her atrocious American accent.

But the man's smile didn't fade. "It's okay. I can speak English." He continued without skipping a beat. "My name is Nhất. Nhất Phán. And this is my son, Duy."

The boy nodded a greeting, not exactly looking back at Freddie. *You-wee*, Freddie repeated in her head. She said the boy's name over and over in her mind, making sure that it would stick in her memory.

Nhất continued, "Your ông ngoại has told me so much about you. You are all he's been able to talk about these last few weeks. He can't even concentrate on his work!"

Ông Ngoại shuffled up to Freddie, giving her a sharp sniff on her temple. "I haven't seen my granddaughter since . . . well, I can hardly remember. That's how long it's been."

Nhất smiled. "You'll be coming to the celebration tomorrow? Guest of honor, obviously."

"Yeah, that's the whole reason I'm here." Freddie felt a warm beat of pride for her grandfather. "Wouldn't miss it."

"Fantastic. Good, good. Very good." Nhất pointed a finger in the air, and with the flick of his wrist, a glistening SUV seemed to appear from nowhere, screeching up to the drive. "It's not every day a man

40

gets recognized for his lifetime achievements. Your ông ngoại is a wonderful, brilliant specimen. One-of-a-kind. I'm very lucky to call him a colleague."

Freddie pressed her head into Ông Ngoại's chest and he sniffed the top of her head.

"Sorry to leave so soon, but I'm afraid my public speaking needs some polishing. I need to practice my speech!" said Nhất as Duy opened the car door for him. But just as Nhất began to step into the car, he turned to look at Ông Ngoại and said, "I look forward to continuing our discussion, old friend."

Ông Ngoại didn't exactly frown, but he didn't exactly smile either. He returned with a sharp nod.

Duy simply nodded as if to say goodbye and followed his father into the fancy car, slamming the door shut behind him. The SUV sped down the street and Freddie watched until it disappeared around a corner.

And then she was left standing in her grandfather's arms. It was the first time coming home felt real.

CHAPTER 4

As everyone started heading into the house, Freddie's mom stopped her at the bottom of the steps.

"Why don't you help Liên bring the bags in?" Mom said in a sharp whisper. Freddie knew from her mother's tone that this was more an order than a suggestion.

Of course, Liên was already back at the car, dutifully unloading suitcases. Liên passed the bags to Freddie and Freddie hauled them inside, then returned again, like they were a well-oiled production line.

With the adults out of earshot, Freddie could finally talk to Liên in private. "I'm really struggling here. I don't think I'm gonna last."

"What do you mean?"

"You heard me back there," said Freddie. "I probably embarrassed Ông Ngoại by not being able to get a single understandable word of Vietnamese out to his friend."

"Ông Ngoại doesn't care about that," said Liên with a wave of her hand. "You're just out of practice. It'll come back to you. I promise. The only thing you can do is keep speaking."

Freddie dragged her hands down her cheeks. "I've forgotten everything."

"You obviously haven't," Liên reassured. "It's easy!"

"Not helpful, Liên."

"Okay, okay. Here's a trick," said Liên. "Vietnamese is a pretty literal language. I mean, like, the Viet word for . . . *vacuum cleaner*. It's *máy hút bụi*. Machine. Sucks. Dirt. Get it? So most of the time if you forget a word or a phrase, you can't go wrong by breaking it down to its most basic form!"

"Not bad," Freddie said, giggling. She had a sudden memory pop up of the word *con chuột túi*. Mouse bag. Or kangaroo.

Inside, it sounded like a party had begun. Freddie and Liên followed the noise to the kitchen, where they found the aunts and uncles catching up. The uncles sat at the long, low tables meant for customers, plucking square ice cubes from a bucket and plopping them into glasses while munching on peanuts and strips of dried squid. Mom and Bác Hoa flitted around enormous vats of bubbling broth, chopping, dicing, tasting sips from the ladle, and chittering away. It came as a shock to Freddie to see her mom work her way around a kitchen— she rarely cooked anything, let alone Vietnamese food.

"Mom?!" Freddie inched her way into the kitchen, careful not to disrupt the chaos. "Since when do you know how to hold a knife?"

"Very funny." Mom fluffed her shirt collar to give herself some relief from the staggering heat. "I was chopping diếp cá when you were still in my belly, ma'am. Literally! Serving canh was my job when I was your age."

"Even younger than that!" hollered Bác Hoa, pushing her way through the kitchen, carrying a neon-green plastic colander overflowing with fish mint leaves. "Your bà ngoại had us in the kitchen as soon as we were old enough to hold a pair of chopsticks."

Bà ngoại, Freddie thought, trying to remember her grandmother, but she came up short. Freddie's bà ngoại had passed away not too long after Freddie was born, and Mom rarely talked about her.

"But when we got to America, I swore my days in the kitchen were over!" Mom laughed. "Now look at me— sucked right back in!"

"I tried to teach Liên how to cook," joked Bác Hoa, stirring a giant pot of rice, "but the poor thing kept breaking dishes and cutting her fingers. She was costing the restaurant money!"

Liên blushed, turned away, and slinked out of the kitchen. Freddie felt a bit of secondhand embarrassment for her cousin. Freddie's aunts and uncles loved to tease, but sometimes they took their jokes too far.

Freddie scanned the room as she stirred a jar of pickled carrots and shallots. Her grandfather was nowhere to be found. She was hoping he'd stick around for a little longer at least.

Mom rinsed a fistful of cilantro leaves as she nodded toward the courtyard. "Honey, if you want to see him, go see him."

That was the push she needed. Freddie headed to the back but turned to find Liên over at the old family piano, playing an Elton John song for the uncles as they sang along. Bác Lộc wasn't much for small talk, but you couldn't keep him away from a karaoke mic. Freddie joined Liên at the piano bench.

"I'm going to go say hi to Ông Ngoại . . ."

"You should!" Liên's fingers flew across the keys. Freddie had a faint memory of Bác Hoa teaching Liên the piano early on. Both of them, actually. Freddie abandoned the piano pretty quickly but Liên had clearly kept up with her lessons.

"Could you, uh . . . come with me? You know . . . my Vietnamese is a little . . . rusty." Freddie's stomach fluttered. She hated asking for help, but this was her first time seeing her grandpa in years. It needed to be perfect.

"Yeah, of course," Liên shut the piano's key lid, and the uncles booed. "But I think you're being too hard on yourself. Your Vietnamese is fine. Push through, remember?"

The cousins made their way to the courtyard. In the center, just under the mangosteen tree, was a crooked, white stone birdbath that gargled water. The old mangosteen tree still bore fruit, so they had to step around the plump, ripe purple spheres that scattered the ground. Freddie hadn't seen a mangosteen in years. They reminded her of little bombs with their bulbous dark purple body and green fuse-like stems.

The cousins reached Ông Ngoại's bedroom. As Ông

Ngoại had gotten older, the family moved his bedroom to the first floor so that he wouldn't have to endure the stairs. Freddie knocked on the door, but there was no answer.

Where was he?

Liên shrugged. "He's been acting kind of weird lately. This whole ceremony is getting to him. Not really hanging around the family as much. He's always in his room, doing 'research.'" She made air quotes on the last part.

Freddie considered abandoning the whole thing and returning to the kitchen but stopped herself. No. She was going in there. She didn't come all this way to chicken out.

Freddie grabbed Liên's wrist and pushed open the door.

A creaky ceiling fan whirled above a humble twin-sized bed. A nightstand held an empty glasses case, a cup of water, and a plate with some mangosteen peels. Bookshelves that reached all the way to the ceiling wrapped around almost every inch of the walls, packed with books. A closer look on one shelf revealed a single black-and-white framed photograph. It was her grandfather in his youth, shirtless and tanned, with a subtle smile. He was posed in front of a small helicopter with a bubble dome. Freddie grew up hearing that her grandfather was once a pilot, but that was the extent of her knowledge.

Aside from the books, there were framed shadow boxes hanging from what little space was left on the walls. One was his degree in history. Another was his degree in archaeology. Some displayed beautiful, pinned butterflies and a colorful assortment of beetles and bugs.

As Freddie inched her way deeper into the bedroom, she stopped in front of the glass cases, remembering the hours she'd spent gazing at all the rocks, necklaces, ancient coins, intricate carved statues, and other various trinkets—things that Ông Ngoại collected over the years during his research excursions. Ông Ngoại was a curator of historic artifacts, but he was especially interested in objects that were related to old stories, legends, and folklore.

"Con có nhớ cái này không?" came her grandfather's voice from behind.

"He's asking you if you remember this stuff," Liên whispered.

"Yeah, I got that much," said Freddie, turning pink.

Then she addressed Ông Ngoại but switched to English, hoping that he'd switch too. "Kind of." She stepped aside, allowing him to gesture to a small, very old-looking curl-toed slipper on the shelf.

"Some say that this is Tấm's slipper from the tale of Tấm and Cám. A story similar to your—Oh, what was it called again?"

"Cinderella?" Liên offered.

"Ah, yes. That's the one." He continued over to a long, thin, corroded sword. "This was a sword once owned by Lê Lợi. Granted, it's not *the* magical sword, Thuận Thiên, but still . . . I was happy to find it."

"Wait, what about this one?" Freddie reached for a beautiful, intricately patterned antique bracelet. A curved, glossy stone as black as onyx dangled from a simple gold chain. "This one looks familiar . . ."

Ông Ngoại laughed. "I'm not surprised. You were always trying to sneak off with that bracelet. One night, you somehow managed to talk your poor cousin into playing the piano to distract me while you slipped right into my room and played dress up. Oh, I was so mad, but you two were so cute that I couldn't stay angry for long. Though I did make you clean my office top to bottom for that little stunt."

Freddie and Liên shared an embarrassed look before bursting out laughing. Still, Freddie struggled to remember, but too much time and distance had passed—the memories were like blurry Polaroids just out of Freddie's reach.

She gently placed the bracelet back in its case and moved on to another glass box suspended on the wall—the only box in the room that was empty. "What's supposed to be in this one?"

"Ah, yes." Ông Ngoại stepped up to it, cleaning his glasses on his shirt. "That one I've been saving for the crossbow."

"What crossbow?" Freddie asked.

"You don't remember?" Ông Ngoại folded his hands behind his back. There was a gleam in his eye. "You used to beg me to recite the legend to you." He turned to Liên. "Both of you did. And I don't blame you—it's quite the story. My favorite, actually."

"Can we hear it?" asked Freddie.

There was that twinkle in his eyes again. "I think I can do that for you, con."

He recounted the tale as if he were back in his old college, giving a lecture—everything from the king begging the gods to protect Âu Lạc, to the golden turtle, to the devastation of the magic crossbow, to the betrayal of the prince and princess, to the engineer stumbling upon the tragic scene on the beach.

Freddie found herself a little girl again, lost in her grandfather's natural gift of storytelling. When he abruptly finished, it was like she was jostled from a dream. She didn't want the story to end.

"What ever happened to Cao Lỗ? Or the baby? Or the crossbow?" asked Freddie. Fairy tales always ended the same way—with more questions than answers.

"No one knows," said Ông Ngoại. "But I'd always hoped to find that crossbow someday. To gaze upon it in that glass case. I spent my whole life searching for it, and now . . ." He trailed off, as if keeping his final thoughts on the matter to himself. "The thing about these old stories is that they shift after being passed down from generation to generation. They evolve. You could say that these legends are a reflection of our own lives. You must adapt. You must pivot. Do you understand what I mean?"

Freddie and Liên looked at each other, both were afraid to admit they had no idea what Ông Ngoại was trying to tell them.

He whipped off his glasses and rubbed his tired eyes.

"Xin lỗi, con. I'm getting tired, I know I'm not making a lot of sense. There's something I'm still working on. Something I need to finish."

"Can I help?" asked Freddie, walking over to him. She wasn't sure exactly what the problem was or even if she had the skillset to assist, but the words came tumbling out.

"No." Ông Ngoại turned to Freddie and gently took both her wrists in his hands, something he used to do all the time when she was little and still in Vietnam. "I don't want you to worry about it."

Freddie wanted to say more, but before she got a chance, he turned around and put his glasses back on.

"I'll be out shortly," he said. "Then we'll have a nice, long talk. I promise."

Liên opened the door for Freddie and guided her out. Freddie stopped at the doorway, desperate to say something to keep the conversation going. But Ông Ngoại was already writing in his journal. There was no use in staying.

"I told you he's been acting weird lately," said Liên, closing the door behind her as they left Ông Ngoại's room. "But we have a whole two weeks ahead of us. Let's try to enjoy it. Don't let him get to you."

"He *is* the point of the whole trip, Liên. What's going on with him, do you think?"

"It's this ceremony," said Liên. "Ever since he told us it was happening, he's been distant. But I know for a fact he's happy you're here."

Liên gave Freddie a sheepish grin, trying to cheer her up, but Freddie frowned. Whatever Freddie was expecting, this definitely wasn't the reunion she was hoping for.

CHAPTER 5

The two Lỗ women had prepared a feast. The uncles moved the restaurant's tables together in a futile attempt to make enough room to hold all the dishes. Steam billowed from a tureen of their family's signature fried fish—cake broth. Bright orange crab sat drenched in thick murky pools of sweet tamarind sauce. There were skewers of plump squid adorned with slices of fresh cucumber and stalks of green onion. A neat pile of shimmering green leaves lay drizzled in dark plum sauce. And in the middle of it all was a whole fish sliced open exposing chunky flakes begging to be dunked in spicy nước chấm. Freddie wasn't used to a spread like this. Back home, most of her meals consisted of takeout.

The tall, empty beer glasses cluttered what little space was left on the table. The adults cheered and threw back their glasses, each one vying to be heard over the others. Freddie strained to keep up with the frantic conversation. Liên had been right. Freddie was getting better at understanding Vietnamese, but it still wasn't great. If everyone would just slow down a bit, it might give her a chance to decipher the chatter. But Vietnamese is not a slow language, and no one patiently waits for another person to finish their thought before jumping right in. At any given moment, three or four different subjects were being discussed at the same time—and loudly.

Now Freddie regretted sneaking off with Tash and Nisa all those weekends she skipped out on her Vietnamese lessons. Her mom had paid good money for her to study Vietnamese from the monks at the local temple along with all the other "good" Viet kids. She wished she could magically swap places with her cousin, who was laughing along, Vietnamese flowing from Liên like the same perfect notes that seemed to waft from her piano, trickling along like a sweet, serene, babbling brook. Whenever Freddie tried to join in, her words felt like choppy, salty waves pounding against a seawall.

Between servings, Freddie kept looking toward the

courtyard, hoping that her grandfather would join them. But he never came, and eventually, she grew tired of waiting. Maybe she'd try to coax him out of his bedroom the next morning, but for now, a warm shower was calling to her. It's not like she was contributing to the conversation anyway.

"Where are you going?" her mom asked as Freddie got up from the table.

"Đi đám," said Freddie, dipping her toes in Vietnamese.

A hush fell over the room. Freddie stiffened; she went cold, then hot all over.

Bác Thanh snorted, unleashing a belly laugh. A smattering of chuckles came up from the other tables.

Liên's hand flew to her mouth, covering a smile. She quickly reset herself and tried tossing Freddie a life preserver. "You're going to . . . a funeral?"

"Bath! I meant that I'm going to take a bath." As Freddie stood there, she could feel a warm, humiliated flush spread across her body. The language was delicate in that way—one accent slip up could change the entire meaning of the word.

"Oh, honey." Freddie's mom reached out to her. "We're not laughing at you. It's cute!"

Cute? Her terrible accent was *cute*? That somehow

made it worse. With her uncle's laugh ringing in her ear, Freddie bolted to the courtyard.

Even though the stars were out and the gentlest of breezes snuck through the branches, the heat from the day lingered. Freddie placed her palm on the mangosteen tree, feeling its rough bark. She wasn't this bumbling wad of embarrassment back home. In fact, Tash and Nisa loved when she would take charge and place everyone's phở orders in Vietnamese. It kind of made her feel like a rock star, being able to show off another language. So why did coming back here make Freddie feel like such a stumbling stranger? She shouldn't have come. She should have stayed home, staying past curfew sipping milk tea with her buddies, laughing and shooting boba at each other through straws, or practicing her drop-ins under the Burnside Bridge. Maybe coming back was a mistake.

Just then, Freddie heard someone approaching. Probably Mom, coming out to comfort her.

"Go away, Mom." Freddie sighed.

No use.

"Mom, I said go awa—"

But when Freddie spun around, she was surprised to find it was Ông Ngoại.

"Hi, con." His heavy eyes watered behind his bifocals. Freddie wasn't sure if he was on the verge of crying or old age or if it was a side effect of the sleepless nights. He reached out a shaky hand, and she took it. "What's wrong, Công chúa Măng cụt?"

Freddie wiped a tear from her eye. "Nothing, Ông Ngoại. It's silly."

Ông Ngoại waited patiently for Freddie to fess up.

"I mixed up my words at dinner . . . and Bác Thanh laughed at me," Freddie admitted. "Everyone laughed at me."

"Pay him no mind, con." Ông Ngoại grunted, waving her off. "Your Bác Thanh could use a Vietnamese lesson himself."

Freddie gave a light chuckle. Even if he was saying that just to make her feel better . . . it was working.

"Come," said Ông Ngoại. "Walk with me."

He led her outside and down the street. Freddie heard that New York City was sometimes called the City that Never Sleeps—well, that could be said for every city and town Freddie had passed through so far in Vietnam. People were still roaming about, gobbling a late-night meal from Styrofoam containers, holding hands as they crossed foot bridges, sitting and chatting at plastic tables, their legs crossed as flip flops dangled from their mani-cured feet.

Despite the bustle of town, Freddie and Ông Ngoại soon found themselves on the beach. In the distance, she could see the rock formation that made up the turtle's head. For a long time, grandfather and granddaughter didn't speak. Freddie, too afraid to spoil the moment, allowed herself to enjoy the evening stroll with her grand-father. He held the crook of her arm, keeping himself balanced, and didn't let go until their feet touched the sand. The beach was empty, except for a few tiny crabs scuttling back into their burrows.

"Do you remember coming here with me?" He said this in Vietnamese, his voice slow and steady, as if he knew Freddie could better understand him that way. "I used to take you with me all the time. You never left my side. Any time I'd try to leave the house, no matter what time it was, even if I was going to exercise at five in the morning, you'd somehow know and come running up to join me. When your mom told us she was moving to America, I knew I'd miss those special hours with you, but I never realized how much."

They were both quiet, taking in the moment.

Then Ông Ngoại chuckled. "The beach was ours.

You used to scare me to death, running straight into the ocean before I could stop you. The waves would knock you over, but you'd always get right back up again." He pointed to a rock formation in the distance. "See those sea caves over there? If I turned my back for a second, you'd be off exploring all the little secret coves and tunnels. I had to beg you to come back before the tide came in."

Like the waves that sloshed over their feet, Freddie suddenly started to remember bit by bit. She had a memory of Ông Ngoại holding her hand as they ordered fresh bánh mì from a cart right on the beach. They'd find a piece of wall to sit on together. Freddie would pluck the slices of jalapeño peppers from her baguette, which Ông Ngoại was happy to relieve her of. Another memory flashed—Freddie filling a bucket with as many seashells as she could find, even if most of them were broken, and proudly showing her bounty to him.

Freddie smiled. "It was so long ago."

"No," he said, staring at the warm waves rolling in. "It was yesterday."

Freddie let the moment linger, squeezing her grandfather's hand. "It's hard for me to remember my life back then. It's like I have little pockets of memories. But they aren't solid. It's like I'm stumbling through a . . . uh . . ." That hot, embarrassing feeling rose as she searched for the right word.

Ông Ngoại smiled. "Sương mù?"

"Yeah. Exactly like fog," said Freddie. The flash of embarrassment disappeared. "It's like I'm walking through fog trying to grasp onto something. Am I home? Am I not home? I'm stuck somewhere in between."

"You know, I gave you that nickname. Princess Mangosteen," he said. "But it wasn't because you gobbled up all the fruit from our tree. Mangosteen is a strange fruit. Very hard to grow. They require perfect soil, the perfect amount of water. They have to have the right balance or they'll die. Mangosteen trees can be stubborn, but if you can care for them by giving them exactly what they need, they'll thrive." Ông Ngoại winked. "You live in America. You may even look a bit like an American. But you'll always be Vietnamese." He put his arm around her and pulled her in tight.

Freddie relaxed into his hug. There was so much she had to tell him, to ask him about, but she didn't want to ruin the moment, and she didn't want it to end.

There would be plenty time to do all that tomorrow.

CHAPTER 6

Freddie woke to the sound of pure chaos. She sat up, wiping the jet lag from her eyes and reorienting herself. Liên wasn't in her bed, which meant that Freddie was the last one to get up. Typical. But today, Freddie actually cared about waking up on time. She peeked out the window, down into the courtyard. Liên was alone, doing . . . something. Dancing? No, it was some kind of routine. Whatever it was, Freddie didn't recognize it. She shook it from her mind—Freddie had other things to worry about. She got dressed, brushed her teeth, threw a comb through her hair, and hustled downstairs.

Everyone was shuffling around the house, preparing for Ông Ngoại's big day. Her mom, Bác Hoa, and the uncles all raced around the house making hurried phone calls and bumping into each other in the crowded kitchen. The stoves never got a break; every second, someone was stirring, searing, or sautéing something. At first, Freddie tried to simply stay out of everyone's way by hovering near one of the tables, picking at a plate of bánh cuốn—a rice noodle roll stuffed with mushrooms, fried shallots, and pork, then drenched in nước chấm. All everyone did was eat, but no matter how many people went back for seconds or thirds, they never made a dent.

Liên came in from outside and immediately started being overly helpful and organized, coordinating with the aunts and working with the uncles to declutter the courtyard and set it up for a grand party. Freddie joined eventually, helping where she could. She wiped down folding chairs before setting them up in tidy rows. Liên and Freddie were in charge of making sure that the speakers were working properly, and they did frequent sound checks on the microphone at the podium. The family set up string lights and hung a colorful array of silk lanterns purchased from their last vacation to Hội An, a picturesque tourist town that was once an old trading port, known for its monthly Lantern Festival. A river carved its way through the town that was the home to a flurry of fishing boats, each one lighting up the night with their paper lanterns. The transformation was enchanting.

And, in an extremely rare occasion, the Lỗ family had closed the restaurant for the day. Liên had to scramble to write a sign explaining to their loyal customers why they were shutting down. She wrote in big block letters—which she then translated for Freddie—that the restaurant would open the next day, after Ông Ngoại's celebration.

Bác Hoa waved Liên over. "We're out of tamarind. Go to the market and pick some up."

"Dạ Mẹ," she said. *Yes, Mom.*

"Oh, and take Freddie with you!"

Liên shrank, tucking a strand of hair behind her ear. "Mẹ, I can walk to the market on my own. It's not like I haven't been there a thousand times."

"I'd feel safer if your cousin was with you."

Liên protested, "I don't understand why I—"

"Pick up some mực too!" Bác Thanh cut her off. "We're out of squid!"

Freddie nudged Liên as they headed deeper into town. "Sorry if I'm barging in on your trip. If you really want to be alone, I'll lie and say that I was with you the whole time. Trust me, I'm not above that."

Liên shook her head. "Obviously I was going to have you come with me. It's just the principle, you know? Like my mom still won't let me go to the stupid market by myself. It's humiliating. It's like they still think I'm a baby. *Your* mom doesn't treat you like that. You get to do whatever you want. Maybe I should start getting Cs and Ds."

"Hey!"

"You know what I mean," said Liên. "You get to do whatever you want. Skateboarding? My parents would never. I'd have to be wrapped in three layers of bubble cushion and have a helmet that could sustain an astronaut's reentry before they'd let me step foot in a skate park. It's not fair."

Freddie could offer only a nod in solidarity. Secretly, she could see where Bác Hoa was coming from—Liên had the superpower (or terrible luck) of getting herself hurt. Freddie could vaguely recall a handful of times she had to carry home a wailing, injured Liên on her back. The family joked that Liên was made of glass. But Freddie could never tell her cousin that.

The market was only a mile away and it was early

enough to enjoy a walk without getting assaulted by the sun. Liên said it was an outdoor market, but that was only partially correct. The first half of the market was outdoors, although it was almost entirely covered by different strips of tarps all thrown together to provide the vendors some protection from the brutal sun. The back half of the market was inside an actual building packed end-to-end with cramped merchant stalls.

Freddie made sure to stick close to Liên; it was easy to get lost in the madness. There was only a single narrow path to navigate the market with. The passageway was choked with customers and tourists, picking their way through pyramids stacked with persimmon fruits or the smooth round balls of longan, or trying to snap pictures. A steady stream of hose water, used to keep the live seafood fresh, trickled down the middle of the walkway. Liên didn't seem to mind it, maybe because her sandals allowed her to step around the man-made river with ease. Meanwhile, Freddie's soggy shoelaces kept slapping the back of her ankles.

The workers tending the stalls watched over their baskets brimming with spiky rambutan as red as fire engines, towers of tofu (both fried and fresh) stacked like bricks, and all sorts of green veggies twinkling with condensation. Silver metal bowls cluttered the ground, housing giant lobsters with long, thin wriggling antennae as well as tiny snails and shucked oysters. Liên had to pull Freddie out of the way of a rolling fish head as an old woman, hunched in a squat and wearing a conical hat and rubber boots, brought down a giant cleaver. This happened more than once.

Wooden crates were packed with flapping, squawking chickens. A rooster with a dark green plumy tail strutted between stalls. Some ladies cackled through gossip, while others kicked back in their folding chairs, checking their phones. Men in sopping wet aprons pushed past the crowds carrying towers of plastic tubs teeming with sealife. Massive speckled crabs tried to scuttle out of ice buckets, only to be casually knocked back in by sun kissed hands. Freddie saw striped shrimp actually leap straight out of their buckets. She didn't even know shrimp could do that!

A peculiar feeling washed over Freddie as they bumped and nudged their way through the crowded market. Every major city had a Chinatown or a Little Saigon, but she couldn't remember ever seeing so many people congregated in one place who looked so much like her. Waves of black hair and brown skin rushed all around her. Suddenly hearing rapid-fire Vietnamese chatter engulf her felt like a comfort blanket. Vietnam was starting to feel a little more like home.

A lady behind a cart pulled Freddie out from her daydream when she beckoned the girls over, her palm facing the ground. A stack of flattened husks was piled high in front of the cart.

"What's she selling?" Freddie asked through a mouthful of a puff pastry Liên had purchased from a vendor working an open charcoal stove.

"You don't remember?"

"Liên, if we're gonna survive this vacation together, you can't ask me that every time we go somewhere."

"Okay, okay," said Liên. "It's like a sugarcane drink. We used to have it all the time. You'd like it!"

"Can you order me one?" Freddie made her best anime eyes.

Liên glared at Freddie from over her glasses, much like her English teacher, Mrs. Bates, when she suspected Freddie knew the answer to a question that she'd gotten wrong.

"Yeah right, Freddie, you can do this. Tell her what you want."

Maybe Liên was right. It wasn't like Freddie to be

this scared. Why was she acting like some timid tourist? She was *born* here!

"Yeah, totally. I was kidding," Freddie said, waving Liên off and turning to the vendor. "Two, uh, drinks please. Two . . ."

Freddie stalled. She knew the Vietnamese words for *sugarcane juice* was tucked deep in the wrinkles of her brain. If she could only remember. Liên was watching her. The vendor was watching her. It felt like the whole market was watching her. Even the rooster seemed to be paying close attention. That's when Freddie remembered Liên's advice—Vietnamese was literal. Break it down to its most basic form. And then:

"Nước mía!" Water. Sugarcane. "Hai cái," Freddie said, holding up two fingers. She winced, praying that she'd gotten the accent right.

The vendor grinned and shoved a stalk of sugarcane between two metal rollers, then turned the wheel crank. A stream of pale yellow juice poured into two cups.

"Hai, ba, dzô!" The cousins raised their plastic cups and toasted in the traditional Viet way.

Liên was right—the sweet juice was delicious and quenching and familiar, like remembering a memory she didn't know she had.

The girls walked together, sipping their drinks. If Freddie had to go back to America tomorrow, she would have been satisfied. Hanging with her cousin after all these years, drinking a sweet sugarcane juice to cool off from the aggressive sun as a cacophony of Vietnamese buzzed in the background. Maybe Freddie could get used to this after all.

"What's going on back in America?" asked Liên, swirling her straw in her cup. "How's it going with all the hanging ten and popping wheelies?"

"I don't know what lingo you picked up, but whatever you said has nothing to do with skateboarding." Freddie laughed. "But to answer what I think your question was, yes, I still enjoy all those activities. What about you? You still, I dunno, getting straight As, reading a thousand books, and killing it at piano recitals or whatever?"

Liên frowned. "There's more to me than books and good grades, you know."

Freddie winced, remembering that she was trying *not* to bring up Liên's academic achievements. She raised her hands in surrender. "Hey, that's a compliment! I'd give anything to be a brainiac like—"

"I'm doing Bà Trà!" Liên interjected, practically

shouting. It was as if she'd been waiting for the perfect moment to reveal this bit of new information. Or maybe it was more like a suspect in an interrogation room cracking under the pressure.

"Bà what-now?" Freddie wrinkled her nose in confusion. "Oh! Is that what you were doing this morning?"

"It's a martial art." Liên pulled a black-and-white checkered scarf from her purse. Freddie noticed a sudden pep in Liên's voice that she hadn't picked up on before. "At first my mom wouldn't let me, no matter how much I begged. But I promised that it wouldn't interfere with my grades or piano lessons, and it hasn't, so she let me. I'm getting pretty good."

Freddie snort-laughed. She really didn't mean to let it slip, but the visual was too much. She couldn't imagine her dainty, bookish cousin getting into any type of fight. And win.

"What's so funny?" Liên frowned.

"Sorry, I'm not laughing. Well, I am, but it's not at you . . ." Freddie felt herself start to sweat and it wasn't because of the humidity. "I had no idea you were into that stuff. Little Liên! Martial arts! You used to cry and run home if you felt seaweed touch your feet."

"Oh, so *now* your memory is coming back." Liên

wrapped her scarf around Freddie's wrist. "I'm telling you—I'm good."

"What are you doing?"

"I'm disarming you."

Liên yanked at the scarf but it slipped off Freddie's wrist. She stumbled backward, which threw Freddie's arm back too, causing juice to splash all over her shirt.

"Liên! I'm covered in sticky juice now! What gives?!"

Liên's cheeks flushed as she wrapped her scarf around her knuckles again. "I didn't do it right. One more try."

Freddie raised her cup in the air, out of Liên's grasp. "No way. I'm not sacrificing any more of my hard-earned nước mía on—"

But something caught Freddie's eye. There, at the far end of the market, was a tall, muscled man who looked very familiar, but Freddie couldn't quite place him. Could it be?

It was. The station agent. But he wasn't in uniform. He wore a tight-fitting polo, beige slacks, and ominous sunglasses. The scowl was the same though.

And he was looking right at them.

Freddie leaned in, speaking from the side of her mouth. "Hey, Liên, I don't want to freak you out, but we have to go. Like, now."

"What? Why?"

"That freaky guy from the train station . . . he's here."

Liên stuffed her scarf back into her purse. "It can't be a coincidence, can it?"

The station agent faced in their direction. But did he actually see Freddie? She couldn't take any chances.

"We shouldn't run, though, right?" Liên said, a quiver in her voice. She tugged the brim of her sunhat low over her eyes. "Then he'll see us for sure. We should walk. But don't walk too slowly."

"I don't even know what that means!" Freddie grabbed her cousin by the wrist and pulled her into the market building. They were clumsy and awkward, squeezing their way around the raucous lunch-hour crowds. Once inside, Freddie found it instantly harder to breathe. They twisted and turned past towering jars filled with peppers, chilies, powdered beef jerky, and dried squid. Liên frantically wiped away droplets of condensation from her glasses when they raced by noodle booths billowing with steam.

Freddie couldn't help herself. She had to take a look, a quick peek, turning her chin over her shoulder. Sure enough, the station agent stared right back at her, shedding his sunglasses. He was moving quicker now in short, deliberate movements, his eyes ablaze.

"We're being followed," said Freddie. "Run!"

The cousins bolted. The station agent picked up his pace to match theirs, shoving patrons aside and sending racks of lacquered rice bowls clattering to the ground.

The market seemed to stretch for miles. They were lost in a maze of merchandise. Where was the exit?

Keep moving. Don't look back. Keep moving, Freddie thought.

Freddie didn't have a route in mind but she tugged Liên's wrist, urging her to move faster. Left here. Right there. Right again. They zigged around the T-shirt stalls then zagged around the belts and wallets section, and down a row of jewelry merchants. They muttered a quick apology when they nearly tripped over a lady selling lottery tickets.

"There!" pointed Liên. "We can get out that way!"

They stumbled out into the light but found themselves on a bridge, facing the water. And even worse, the station agent was hot on their tails. He emerged from around the building, eyes locked on the cousins, and made a beeline for them.

"What are we gonna do?" asked Liên, looking around frantically.

"I don't know, I—"

Just then, and seemingly out of nowhere, an onyx motorcycle with hornet-yellow stripes skid in front of the girls, forcing them to jump back. The driver wore a black helmet with the visor pulled down.

They revved their engine. "Hop on!"

"Who are you?!" Freddie's hands snapped up reflexively, balling into fists like a boxer poised to strike.

"We need to go. He's almost here."

"Who?"

"Con Hổ."

"The Tiger," Liên translated, sensing Freddie's confusion.

This was the first time a proper translation didn't make Freddie feel better.

The station agent—Con Hổ—broke out into a sprint.

Freddie and Liên looked at each other, out of options, then scrambled onto the back of the bike. Freddie took the middle and Liên wrapped her arms around Freddie's waist. She had no idea who Con Hổ was or why he was chasing them, but the mysterious motorcyclist felt like the better gamble.

"Grab onto me," said the driver, sensing Freddie's hesitation. Freddie picked up a hint of annoyance in his voice. She squeezed her eyes shut and put her hands on his hips. It had been a while since she'd been on the back of a motorcycle, and never with a stranger.

The driver knocked the kickstand with their foot and the motorbike with hornet-yellow stripes peeled out, sending gravel flying in every direction. Freddie adjusted her grip, fearing she'd tumble off at any second.

It became obvious that their mystery driver didn't seem to know what brakes were. They whipped the bike away from the busy market, spilling out onto the streets.

"Move!" they shouted at passersby, blasting the horn. "Get out of the way!"

Freddie thought for sure they'd hit a pothole that would send them skittering into traffic. But the driver knew how to maneuver a bike and they managed to swerve, barely missing food carts and bouncing off of narrow alley walls.

"Can you, like, turbo boost this thing?" yelled Freddie.

"I'm pushing it as much as I can!" the driver hollered back.

By the time they reached another bridge overlooking a sparkling bay, Con Hổ was only a figure in the distance. Still, he caused Freddie to shudder.

When they'd gotten far away enough from the market, the driver stopped the bike to let the cousins off. Luckily, they weren't too far away from the house, which was a good thing because Freddie's arms ached from gripping so tightly.

The driver dismounted first before helping Freddie and Liên down.

"You going to take your helmet off, or at least tell us who you are?" Freddie's head was spinning, and it wasn't because of their roller-coaster ride through the market. She had a thousand questions, all of which deserved answers. Who was this motorcycle guy? Who was Con Hổ? Why was he after Freddie?

The driver got back on the motorcycle.

Liên pulled off her glasses, inspecting the lenses for any cracks. "Okay, then how about you tell us who Con Hổ is and why he's after us."

The driver spun the bike around, revving his engine. "Ask your ông ngoại."

And with that the driver was gone.

CHAPTER 7

The girls raced to the house, still processing what exactly had happened back at the market.

"What are we going to do?" Liên gripped her sunhat so that it wouldn't fly off.

"We find Ông Ngoại, I guess." Freddie shook her head, hoping to shake loose some of the confusion.

As they approached the house, the girls gasped. Everything looked completely transformed. From the looks of it, you'd think the Lỗs were hosting a Hollywood awards show. A massive red carpet stretched from the front doors to the street, which was flooded with cars and vans. Not only were the guests arriving, but Freddie took note that rows of unmarked black sedans choked the surrounding alleyways. A valet station was set up, and valets in matching polo shirts and shorts raced about, parking cars and opening doors for guests.

"Oh man, we're super late." Freddie asked as a valet rushed past her.

Liên sidestepped, narrowly avoiding another valet. "I guess Nhất decided to cater the event himself? I knew he had money, but not *this* much money."

The cousins walked inside to a whirlwind of preparation. The first floor of the house was already flooded with guests greeting each other. Finely dressed caterers poured from the kitchen, plating food on the folding tables set out around the courtyard. It seemed like all of Võ Rùa Làng was here. Friends, neighbors, pretty much anyone who knew Ông Ngoại shuffled into the courtyard to take their seats, some wearing their finest suits and dresses.

Freddie caught sight of Nhất, the host for the afternoon, under the mangosteen tree, directing some of his hired help to clear out the fallen fruit. "Careful now to get every single piece. You don't want to get any juice on your clothes or it'll never come out. Trust me."

Mom tapped Freddie on the shoulder. She was wearing a modest white skirt and white top with matching earrings, but it was the most dressed up Freddie had ever seen her. "Where have you two been? Bác Lộc and Bác Hoa have been worried sick about Liên!"

"The market! We had to get . . ." Freddie felt her face fall as realization struck her.

"Oh, no!" Liên said. "We forgot to get the tamarind and the squid!"

"It doesn't matter," said Mom with the wave of her hand. Freddie detected a bit of annoyance in her voice. "Nhất surprised us by bringing enough food to feed this entire town and then some."

"Just wish he would have mentioned that to us before we spent all morning cooking," grumbled Bác Hoa, walking by carrying a stack of dishes. She snapped her attention back to the cousins. "You two need to get dressed! Hurry! The ceremony is about to begin."

Freddie blinked. "Dressed?" Uh-oh.

Mom took one look at Freddie and Freddie knew was in for it. "Don't tell me . . ."

"I kinda . . . sorta . . . forgot to pack—"

"Freddie, how could you?" Mom said. "You know how important today is!"

"It's okay!" Liên interjected. "I have an extra áo dài she can wear!"

Mom shook her head. "You should be thankful you have a responsible cousin like Liên."

"Yeah, yeah." Even if Freddie was grumbling about the comparison, deep down she really was grateful that Liên rescued her from another lecture.

"What about Motorcycle Guy?" Liên whispered to Freddie. "We need to talk to Ông Ngoại, remember?"

"What was that?" Mom asked, suspicious.

"Nothing!" Freddie exclaimed. "I mean . . . nothing. Come on, Liên, we're late enough as it is!" She grabbed her cousin's arm and whisked her away.

Upstairs, Liên laid out her áo dài—a traditional, sort-of-fancy Vietnamese dress and silk pants combination worn on special occasions like weddings, funerals, and New Year's. It was a dark crimson accentuated with stitched yellow patterns. She dug deep into her closet and pulled out a pale yellow-and-white áo dài with a floral motif in the center. This áo dài was a bit short in places because Liên had outgrown it.

"Don't forget these," said Liên, tossing Freddie a pair of white chiffon pants.

Freddie slipped on the yellow áo dài and put on the pants. She couldn't picture herself wearing a traditional Vietnamese dress. Even if it was made of silky material,

Freddie squirmed as if there were a phantom itch. "I dunno . . ."

Liên pulled Freddie over to the mirror. "We used to dream about wanting to wear these!"

"*Me?* I said those words?" Freddie twisted and turned, considering herself in the mirror. "Doesn't sound like me."

"You look great. Come on. You can wear this." Liên stepped behind Freddie and softly pushed on her lower back so that she was standing straight and confident. The more Liên spoke, the more Freddie bought into it. "Needed a little posture adjustment, that's all."

Freddie looked at her arms. The áo dài's sleeves stopped at her elbows, not reaching down to her wrists like Liên's. It wasn't quite right.

"It's still missing something," mumbled Freddie. "Don't you think?"

"What do you have in mind?"

Freddie snapped her fingers. "I've got an idea."

Liên looked out the window. Everyone was starting to take their seats. "Hurry up. They're gonna start any second!"

"I'll meet you down there!"

Freddie raced downstairs and slipped into Ông

Ngoại's bedroom. She'd remembered the beautiful brown antique bracelet speckled with red dots. Freddie didn't think he'd kick up *too* much of a fuss if she borrowed this bracelet—not for today, anyway. It was for his own ceremony, after all. She snapped the bracelet around her wrist. A perfect fit.

That's when she heard the door open. Before Freddie knew what she was doing, she was hiding under the bed. *This is silly*, she thought. Feeling a bit foolish, she was about to reveal herself to her grandfather when she realized it wasn't Ông Ngoại who had entered the room.

It was Nhất. He wore a black tuxedo with a red bow tie around his neck. The suit had tails—an odd, slightly outdated choice for evening wear, but Nhất's confidence pulled it off. Not a wrinkle in sight.

Freddie froze, keeping quiet. *What is he up to?*

Nhất carefully thumbed through the books on the shelf before moving over to the glass cabinets.

"Where *is* it?" he whispered anxiously, every so often pausing to eye the door before resuming his search. It was obvious that whatever Nhất was doing, he didn't want anyone else knowing.

Is he ... trying to steal one of Ông Ngoại's artifacts?!

But when Nhất gave up his search of the cabinets, he moved over to the writing desk. After shuffling though papers, Nhất slammed his fist on the desk sending papers flying everywhere.

The noise startled Freddie—so much so that she jolted, thumping her head on the bed.

"Ow!" Freddie said, revealing her presence.

Nhất froze in place. "Who's there?"

Freddie cursed under her breath. She had no choice but to come out of hiding.

"Hi, hello, chào," said Freddie, getting to her feet.

"Oh, Freddie, it's you," Nhất placed his hand over his chest. "You scared me. What are you doing here, con?"

"What are *you*?" It came out with a bit more sass than Freddie intended.

"Touché." Nhất flashed another one of his charming smirks. "Your ông ngoại asked me to collect something for him. That old leather diary he's always carrying around."

"Haven't seen it."

Nhất shrugged. "He must be mistaken, then. Oh, well, I'm sure it will turn up." He grinned, patting her shoulders. A shiver ran up her spine. "The Lỗs certainly know how to dress for an occasion. I saved seats for you and your cousin right up at the front. This is so exciting. Come, come. We're starting."

He led her to the packed courtyard. Not a single empty seat was available, except for the one next to Liên as Nhất had promised. At the far side of the yard was an elevated stage. A row of finely dressed men and women sat straight in their chairs, legs crossed and hands folded. At the very end of the row sat Ông Ngoại, looking stern and serious. When Freddie took her seat, he looked right at her. He didn't smile, but he snuck her a little wink.

Freddie surveyed the courtyard. All the lanterns they'd spent the morning hanging up were gone. So were the twinkle lights. "What happened to all the stuff we worked our butts off to put up?"

Liên shrugged. "I guess Nhất wanted something more sophisticated. And he's not wrong. Everything does look a lot more . . . polished."

"Polished and boring," said Freddie.

"Shhh," Liên whispered. "It's about to start."

Nhất took the podium, a brilliant smile plastered on his face. "I want to thank everyone for coming out for this very special afternoon. We're here tonight to celebrate and acknowledge Dr. Thu, a man whose lifetime achievements have far succeeded even the highest expectations, and who I am convinced will one day go down in Vietnam's history as one of the country's greatest scholars."

The crowd applauded. Freddie made sure she clapped the loudest.

"For those who don't know me, my name is Nhất Phán, and I've had the honor of working alongside the man-of-the-hour for many years. His drive and his passion for our country's history and folklore are unparalleled. I hope that he continues his work for many years to come."

More applause.

"But don't take my word for it," Nhất continued. "I'd like to introduce some of Ông Thu's distinguished colleagues from the course of his career to speak a few words about why we are honoring this man today."

One by one, professors and curators took the mic and each gave a speech about Ông Ngoại. They said more or less the same thing, all gushing about how he influenced their lives and their work. Freddie struggled to understand everything that was said, but still, she could feel a sense of pride in her grandfather swell. She always knew that he was an important man but had no idea he was this beloved by his community.

As the speakers continued, Freddie scanned the courtyard, looking for something to distract her until it was time for her grandfather's entrance. Suddenly, something from the corner of her eye caught her attention. It was Nhất, and he was talking to Duy. Well, not so much talking as . . . berating?

"Where have you *been*?" Nhất spat, jabbing Duy with his pointer finger. "Do you know . . ."

But that was all Freddie could hear because Nhất quickly changed his composure and lowered his voice when a caterer passed by them. Freddie marveled at how quickly Nhất could switch his demeanor at the snap of a finger. Still, Duy kept his head bowed, not saying a word.

Freddie wanted to listen in more, but she forgot all about Nhất and Duy when Ông Ngoại took the stand. Ông Ngoại smoothed his wild hair as best he could as more applause filled the courtyard.

"Cảm ơn, everyone. Thank you." Ông ngoại waved his hands, signaling for everyone to sit. "Before I begin, I'd like to thank my generous host and benefactor. Ông Phán is truly a patron of Vietnamese culture and history. Without his generosity and support, I couldn't have pursued my work—my passion. Thank you."

Applause rose once again from the audience. Some in

the crowd even stood. Nhất, who stepped back into the courtyard, returned with a gracious bow and raised a humble hand, allowing Freddie's grandfather to continue.

Ông Ngoại lowered the mic to account for his short stature. "I'd like to apologize ahead of time. I'd written a much more charismatic speech, but I seem to have misplaced my diary."

Freddie sat up a little straighter. Had Nhất found it? No, he couldn't have; he was here with all the guests this whole time. Could he have been telling the truth after all? Still . . . if Nhất didn't have the diary, and Ông Ngoại didn't have the diary, then . . . where was it?

Ông Ngoại cleared his throat. "When I began my career, you couldn't find a university anywhere that had a class dedicated to Vietnamese folklore. I had to beg the department of history at the university to recognize the importance of studying our country's stories. I had to plead to be taken seriously. Most people think of fairy tales, legends, and folklore as something designed for children—bedtime stories passed down from generations to help them go to sleep at night.

"But I believe that these stories play a deeper role in our lives—an often unappreciated role. I've arguged that folklore say more about us as a people than history books filled with facts. They hold our dreams. They hold our ideals. Over the course of my career, I've learned that some of the best legends have something to say. They're cautionary tales that teach little ones to avoid dangerous scenarios. They teach us to respect our past as we make way for the future. They teach us to be humble, to respect nature, to care for the weak—to stand up for our principles, no matter what."

Freddie looked around to see everyone in the audience nodding in agreement, hanging on Ông Ngoại's every word. He sure knew how to command attention.

"Many of you here tonight have at some point or another heard me prattle on about my analysis of 'The Raven's Gem' or 'The Legend of the Mountain Lord and the Sea Lord.' But perhaps my favorite is the tale of the crossbow. It's gone by many names over time— the Legend of the Saintly Crossbow, Nỏ Thần, The Crossbow of the Golden Claw, and so on and so forth. However, the one constant about that tale is how the crossbow's very existence tore apart friends, families, and soulmates. It's best known for being a tragic love story. But for me, it's always been so much more than that. Which is why I've given the crossbow a name that

I have always felt was more fitting—Nỏ Định Mệnh."

Freddie nudged Liên. "Crossbow of what?"

"Of fate," Liên whispered back. "Like . . . destiny."

"Oh. Got it." Freddie sat back in her chair.

"The legend of Nỏ Định Mệnh is a cautionary tale with a warning that has echoed over thousands of years—the story of how King An Dương succumbed to a lust for power, which led to his own demise and the tragic end to his family. Such a gruesome ending could have been avoided." Ông Ngoại adjusted his glasses. "Now, I want you to imagine yourself as Cao Lỗ, the royal engineer, holding both the turtle claw and crossbow in hand as the bodies of his corrupted best friend, the brave princess, and the lovesick prince stained the sand red with their blood. Standing there, he somehow was able to muster these words. Words that he hoped would resonate. That our people would learn from for generations to come."

Ông Ngoại looked out at the crowd as if he were making eye contact with every single person in the audience.

"Look at all this death. All this destruction. And for what? They shall never be together again."

He shifted his focus, looking right at Freddie. For a

second, his gaze locked on her bracelet before he continued.

"I've been lucky enough to travel up and down our magnificent country, studying its history, its culture. I've seen more than most people could ever dream to in a lifetime. During my expeditions, I may not have ever come across Lê Lợi's magical sword or discovered Dã Tràng's magic pearl, but the experiences and friendships I've made throughout my lifetime of trying to uncover these artifacts are more valuable than the artifacts themselves."

He raised a shaky finger. "Just yesterday, I was telling my granddaughters that legends are shared over many lifetimes and in the course of their retellings, they transform—they evolve. And while the details of these folktales may change, their core messages remain intact. I'd like to think that my life—my career—has reflected the same ebb and flow of these stories. When I first began my journey many, many years ago . . . I sought out fortune and glory. But now, in my old age, surrounded by my family, my granddaughters, I find myself yearning for something more than snatching up ancient relics. It is time for rest."

Whispers erupted in the crowd. Freddie and Liên

looked at each other in confusion. Clearly this was a surprise sprung on everyone.

"I am announcing my official retirement tonight," Ông Ngoại declared.

A hush came over the crowd. A stunned silence.

"Thank you all for attending this special day. Truly, it means so much to me that you all recognize the importance my research has on our country and our culture." Ông Ngoại let out a nervous chuckle before continuing. "I'm looking forward to spending time with my family, especially my granddaughters. I want to thank Nhất and his foundation again for all the support throughout my career. Cảm ơn nhiều."

Freddie whipped around to see how Nhất was taking the news. To Freddie's surprise, Nhất was the first to stand and applaud, which began rippling through the audience. But as Nhất continued to clap, Freddie noticed that his smile wasn't really a smile at all. It wasn't a frown either. It was something else.

By the time Freddie checked back at her grandfather, he had stepped off the stage and retreated back into his room.

CHAPTER 8

The after-party kicked into high gear. Waiters swarmed the crowd carrying platters of even more food and trays balancing extravagantly prepared cocktails. Freddie strained to keep track of Nhất. He was flitting about, whispering to the caterers, and he had two men flanking him at all times. The warm smile she had attributed to him had all but faded, and in its place was a permanent scowl. After discovering Nhất in Ông Ngoại's room, Freddie had a feeling deep in her gut that something wasn't quite right. She was determined to not let Nhất out of her sight.

But hours later, after the party had died down and everyone had gone to bed, Freddie was no closer to catching Nhất in any kind of trap. From the courtyard, leaning against the old mangosteen tree, Freddie fiddled with the bracelet. She watched Nhất give his formal goodbyes, then make his way to Ông Ngoại's room.

A tap on Freddie's shoulder jolted her from nodding off. It was Liên, who was now delicately ripping a chả giò in half. "What's going on? You're acting weird. Like weirder than usual."

"Something weird *is* going on, but it's not me, Liên."

Liên blew the steam away, braving a nibble. "I know. I can't believe Ông Ngoại is actually retiring. He always said you'd have to pry his archaeologist spade from his dead hands!"

"No, I don't mean that. I mean *that*." Freddie nodded in the direction of Ông Ngoại's room. "I think that Nhất guy is up to something. You know before the ceremony when I went to grab this bracelet? I caught Nhất snooping around Ông Ngoại's room."

Liên snapped her fingers. "I always knew there was something off about that guy! What was he looking for?"

"Ông Ngoại's journal."

Liên's nose wrinkled in confusion. "What's so important about that old thing?"

"I don't know, but I have to find out." Freddie started toward the room.

"Wait a second." Liên tugged at Freddie's elbow. "You're not leaving me behind. He's my grandpa too."

Freddie nodded, but she wasn't sure that was such a good idea. Liên wasn't exactly known for her stealthiness, especially given her clumsy Bà Trà demonstration back at the market. Besides, Freddie wouldn't forgive herself if something happened to her cousin.

"Stick close to me." Freddie relented, leading Liên up to Ông Ngoại's door. But before she could knock, she heard talking. No, not talking. *Arguing.* "Let's go around," she whispered.

They tiptoed the outside of the house, pushing through shrubbery and creeping right up to the backside of Ông Ngoại's bedroom.

"Oh great," said Liên, brushing dirt and leaves off her áo dài. "My mom is going to kill me."

"Shhh," said Freddie. "I can hear them."

The girls crouched low and leaned in. Through the window, they spotted Ông Ngoại at his desk. Nhất stood over him. One of the men in suits blocked the door; the other stood directly behind Ông Ngoại.

"That was quite the announcement," said Nhất,

pacing with his hands folded behind his back. "I don't remember hearing *that* part of your speech in rehearsals."

"Xin lỗi," said Ông Ngoại. "But I've made my decision."

"Không." Nhất stepped forward, shaking his head. "No. You don't get to decide when to quit. Not when we're so close. You know what I think? I think you know exactly where the crossbow is and suddenly you've gotten cold feet."

Freddie and Liên shared a look. Crossbow? He couldn't mean the crossbow from the old legend, could he?

Ông Ngoại placed his hands on his desk, palms down, as if to steady himself. "I wanted to find Nỏ Định Mệnh just as much as you do. I've dedicated my entire life to finding it. You know this. It simply doesn't exis—"

"Liar!" Nhất slammed his fist down. Even though Freddie knew it was coming, she still jumped.

Liên turned to Freddie. Her eyes flashed with fear. "We shouldn't be doing this. Let's go tell someone."

Freddie waved her off. "In a minute."

"I'm telling you, I was wrong," Ông Ngoại continued. "I've had to accept it, and so do you. Nỏ Định Mệnh is a myth."

"Never say those words to me!" Nhất snatched Ông Ngoại's trembling chin in his hand. "Don't lie to me again, Thu. You know where the crossbow is and you're going to take me there."

Ông Ngoại shot up from his seat. "Even if I knew where it was, maybe it wasn't meant to be found. If Nỏ Định Mệnh does indeed exist, it should remain hidden. We're meddling in something that could have grave consequences. We have no idea what it's capable of."

"Well," Nhất stepped back and bowed his head. "We're about to find out." The man standing behind the desk grabbed Ông Ngoại's shoulders, while the other went to lock the bedroom door.

Something in Freddie snapped as she saw the scared look in her grandfather's eyes. She wasn't about to sit back and do nothing. Before she even knew what she was doing, and before Liên could stop her, Freddie rushed into the room.

"Let him go!" Freddie shouted, slamming her fists into the muscled bodyguard.

"Ah, I was wondering when you might join us, con," Nhất said coolly. "Don't forget the other one." The man by the door snatched Liên before she could make a run for it. "Then go turn up the music. Order the waiters to pour another round. It's a party, after all. We wouldn't want any more . . . eavesdroppers."

"*Please,*" begged Ông Ngoại. "Leave my grand-daughters alone."

"You have the power to make this all go away," Nhất bargained, scanning the room. Finally, his eyes landed on their target. Carefully, he retrieved Lê Lợi's sword from its case and pointed its thin blade at Freddie. "Tell me what I want to know."

"Don't!" pleaded Freddie.

For a moment, the room fell silent. Ông Ngoại's frightened eyes met Freddie's, then shifted to Liên, then back to Freddie. She could sense he was in an impossible position.

"Đà Nẵng," Ông Ngoại said finally, and sagged. "It's in Đà Nẵng."

"See?" Nhất tsked. "I knew we could reach a compromise."

"You've got what you want. Now go," Ông Ngoại said.

"Not quite yet, old friend. Đà Nẵng is a big city, and I need an insurance policy." Nhất eyed Freddie and Liên. "Throw the eavesdroppers into the van. The old man will ride with me."

A moment later, one of the catering vans backed up to the balcony. Once Freddie and Liên's hands were bound with twine, they were tossed in the back.

"Let us go!" Liên shouted.

"What she said!" Freddie added. "Where are you—"

But Freddie never got to finish her sentence because the last thing she saw before the van's doors closed was— Con Hổ.

CHAPTER 9

It took Freddie a moment to blink awake. She must have dozed off, and she had no idea for how long. Her brain scrambled to catch up to the scenario she found herself in. They were in the back of a catering van, that's all Freddie knew. Stacked wooden crates and cardboard boxes bulging with fruit swayed back and forth. Her body was sore from being twisted in an awkward position for so long. Her wrists ached, still bound by rope. How were they going to get out of this?

Her heart dropped. Where was Liên? Freddie spotted Liên sitting across from her, still asleep. Liên looked like a limp doll left out in the rain. A cold, panicked dread swept over Freddie. Was Liên okay? Was her little cousin even alive?

Freddie frantically kicked Liên with the toe of her sandal until her cousin stirred awake.

"Stop! Stop! I'm awake. I'm *awake!*" mumbled Liên. "What's happening?"

Relief washed over Freddie. "Oh, nothing," she said, trying to twist her wrists out of the twine. It only made the ropes dig into her skin. "Taking a lovely drive through the countryside. Nhất thought we might do some sightseeing in Đà Nẵng. Maybe see the Dragon Bridge, take a food tour, taste some of their famous chè, or, I dunno, maybe see if we can unearth an ancient, mythological crossbow."

Liên sat up. "Where's Ông Ngoại?"

"No idea. He's probably with Nhất, though" said Freddie. "Liên, we gotta get out of here."

Liên shook her head. "I told you we shouldn't have tried to sneak around—"

"What?!" Freddie remembered to lower her voice. "I distinctly remember you wanting to tag along."

"*Tag along?* So now I'm your poor, pathetic little puppy?" said Liên. "What I *said* was that we should have gone for help."

"I'm *sorry*, all right." Freddie allowed herself to take a breath. Apparently that helps in these situations, or so she'd always seen in movies. "Now will you please use that brain of yours to think of something?"

"What do you want me to do?" Liên raised her voice. "You want me to math my way out of this? I'm scared too, Freddie!"

"Okay, okay," said Freddie. "First we need to get our hands back. I think I wiggled some of it loose, but I need like a little branch or a pencil or something thin to wedge a gap in this knot."

"What about that crate at the top there?" asked Liên. "Maybe we can break a piece off."

"Liên, you're a gen—"

"Don't say it."

"It was a compliment, but o . . . kay." Freddie shrugged. Apparently even telling Liên she was smart was off-limits.

Liên shook her head, annoyed, then she used her frustration to kick the boxes over. The tower toppled, but before Freddie could move out of the way, it came crashing down on top of her. For a second, everything went black, followed by tiny little bursts of white light. She finally understood what it meant to see stars.

"Are you okay?" asked Liên, trying to sit up to get a better look. "Are you hurt? Are you bleeding? What was it?"

A searing pain throbbed over Freddie's eye. What got her? A sharp corner of a box? No, something . . . spikey.

"No, I think I got beamed by . . ." Freddie kicked at the culprit—a mutant beast of a durian, a tropical yellow fruit the size of a watermelon, with spikes as long as AAA batteries. "Fruit?"

The cousins looked at each other, bemused. Then Liên snorted, which, of course, caused Freddie to laugh too. Soon the cousins were laughing so hard, they were sweating.

"Okay, okay!" said Freddie, shaking her head. "Stop laughing so we can focus on getting out of here, please!"

"You first!" Liên managed to get out.

Now that the crate was at ground level, Freddie could bust it apart. After a few good kicks, the wood splintered. Freddie wriggled her way over to a bit of wood, about the size of a chopstick, and slipped it into the hole in the knot. She tugged until the knot loosened, but it snagged on her bracelet for a moment. All she had to do was loop the rope around it and . . .

"Voilà!" Freddie massaged her wrists. It felt good to be free from the twine. She started on Liên's bindings next.

"Hmm . . ." said Liên, looking around the van. To Freddie, it seemed almost as if Liên was trying to solve a puzzle in her mind. Finally, her eyes landed on something.

Freddie stared at her cousin, confused, but obeyed. "What are you thinking?"

"That durian gives me an idea," Liên said. "Quick! Act like you're really sick—like you're gonna puke."

Freddie felt a little foolish, but she had a feeling she knew where Liên was going with this. She began with a whimper.

"I know you know how to fake being sick based on how much you've played hooky!" Liên teased.

"Fine, but I don't appreciate what you're insinuating." Freddie gave it her all, groaning even louder, doubling over, and clutching her stomach even though no one but her cousin could see her.

"What's going on back there?" came a muffled voice from the driver's cab.

Liên cupped her hands around her mouth. "I think

my cousin ate some bad nem nướng cuốn back at the party."

"There's no way," said another voice from the cab. "I helped make those nem nướng cuốn myself."

Liên rolled her eyes. "Well, you're not seeing what I'm seeing, and it's about to get real messy back here, so I suggest you let us out for bathroom breaks."

They waited. For a moment, Freddie worried that Liên's plan might not work. "Do you think I should throw in some *trời ơi's*?"

"Yes," said Liên. "Definitely!"

"Oh my god," moaned Freddie. "Trời ơi! Trời ơi!"

"It's the American," said the man up front. "She sounds terrible. And I don't just mean her accent."

Freddie grit her teeth. Now it was personal. Even the bad guys were taking potshots at her Vietnamese! Liên ushered her to keep going. No time to be humiliated about her thick American accent. "I think I'm gonna barf. It's coming. I can feel it! Trời ơiiiiii!"

There was a long pause. Freddie worried that Liên's plan might not work after all. But then, she heard the voice of the driver. "We need to be quick about this or the other cars will get too far ahead of us."

"Did you hear that, Freddie?" Liên whispered, taking

her place near the van's backdoor. "I bet you anything Ông Ngoại is in one of those cars with Nhất!"

Freddie nodded. She felt the van lurch to the side of the road. The pit stop they needed.

"Liên! Hand me that durian!"

Liên kicked the pointy fruit over. Freddie held her breath, took a crouched position by the front door, and held the durian above her head.

"One . . ." Freddie began.

A key slid into the lock from the outside.

"Two . . ." Liên continued.

The lock of the door unlatched.

"Three!" they shouted in unison.

The door swung open. For a split second, Freddie found herself staring back at Con Hổ. It all happened so fast, Freddie didn't have time to chicken out. She heaved the spikey durian, hitting Con Hổ in the face. Con Hổ yowled and collapsed to the pavement.

"Run!" yelled Freddie. The girls leapt from the truck and took off sprinting down the road. Freddie had no idea where they were. Nothing looked familiar. There was only road, a guard rail, and jungle surrounding them. She didn't know where she was leading Liên—all she knew was that they needed to keep running.

"Freddie, they're coming this way!" Liên pumped her arms as she ran. Freddie was surprised how fast Liên could run in an áo dài. The other passenger helped Con Hổ to his feet. Then the two men both started down the road, pointing. And they looked mad. Very mad.

Freddie almost grabbed Liên and planned to leap over the side of the guardrail. A fall would be better than having to face an angry Con Hổ.

But it was a risk she they wouldn't have to take. Just down the road, Freddie heard something: The familiar growl of a motorbike engine—and it was headed straight toward them.

Motorcycle Guy didn't slow down. Freddie pulled Liên out of the bike's path as it barreled ahead. Con Hổ and the other man seemed to be just as surprised by the motorcyclist, because they too jumped to the side to avoid being clipped. Everyone watched, waiting to see what he would do.

The motorcyclist threw his foot out, spinning the bike to a stop next to the truck. With the flick of his wrist, he whipped out a switchblade and sunk it deep into a tire. The truck began to sink, lopsided, as the air from the punctured tire hissed. Then, before anyone could really get a grasp on what exactly was happening,

Motorcycle Guy revved his engine and backtracked toward Freddie and Liên.

"Don't just stand there!" Con Hổ shouted. "Do something!"

Con Hổ's accomplice reached out to grab the driver, but Motorcycle Guy swerved at the last second to avoid his grasp. Now, Motorcycle Guy set his sights on Con Hổ. For a moment, he and Con Hổ just sat there, each sizing up the other, waiting to see who would make the first move. Finally, Motorcycle Guy revved his engine once more and made a beeline for Con Hổ. Freddie noticed that Con Hổ dug his heels deeper into the ground, bracing himself.

Five . . .

Did Motorcycle Guy plan to run him over?

Four . . .

Would Con Hổ move out of the way?

Three . . .

Well. They were going to die.

Two—

And then, at the last moment, Motorcycle Guy lifted up the front of his bike, raising the front wheel while balancing expertly on the back tire. Con Hổ made a grab for the left, but Motorcycle Guy leaned right, the two just barely missing each other. The driver used the opening to zip over to the girls, swerving into a sideways slide that landed inches from Freddie and Liên before settling.

"Are you two crazy?!" said Motorcycle Guy. Yep, this was definitely the same guy from the market. "What are you doing in the middle of the road? And what have you done to your áo dàis? Never mind. Get on—quickly!"

That was enough for Freddie, and the cousins scrambled aboard the bike.

"Uh . . . you guys?" Liên gestured behind her. "What's Con Hổ doing?"

Con Hổ had recovered from his fall and retrieved something from the truck's cab. It was long and metallic. Freddie could make out a glint of something reflecting the moonlight.

"Duck!" yelled Motorcycle Guy, kicking the bike into gear.

There was a loud crack. Something whizzed past Freddie's head.

"Is he . . . *shooting* at us?!" Freddie cried.

"Not great," said Motorcycle Guy. The bike flew even further down the road, and before long, Freddie could barely make out the van, let alone Con Hổ.

Freddie allowed herself to take a breath. "I think we're far enough away now."

"Don't get too comfortable," warned Motorcycle Guy. "That's a hunting rifle, and Con Hổ is a crack shot. Hang on."

Another bang. The driver gripped the handle bars, squeezing the brakes and causing the bike to swerve. A bullet blew away a side mirror, throwing off the bike's balance. Suddenly the bike slammed into the loose gravel and catapulted the riders off the bike. Freddie bounced off the road, gravel chewing up the side of her áo dài, before she finally settled.

Motorcycle Guy rushed over to Freddie, helping her up. "Is everyone okay?"

"Ribs can grow back, right?Freddie said, standing. "Wait. Where's Liên?!"

"I'm okay," winced Liên, scrambling to her feet. "I can walk."

Motorcycle Guy squeezed the bike's front lever. "Good, because we don't have a choice. The brakes are shot."

"What?!" said Freddie. "What are we going to do now?"

"First, we need to get off the road before Con Hổ

catches up to us." Motorcycle Guy picked up the bike. "Quick. Help me with this. Maybe we can take cover in the jungle."

Together, they rolled the bike through a small gap in the guardrail. There was no other option in the time they had. They were going deeper into the jungle, which was certainly better than facing Con Hổ.

"Keep going," Motorcycle Guy urged. "We need to put as much distance between us and Con Hổ as we can." He pulled something out of a pouch on the side of the bike—a machete. "Who wants brush clearing duty?"

Just before Liên could grab it, Freddie stepped in and claimed the machete first. "*I'll* take that." Liên swinging an enormous, sharp blade was just asking for trouble.

Liên stopped walking, putting her hands on her hips. "Um, I've got questions. Lots of questions."

"I suggest we save those for later," said Motorcycle Guy without looking back. "Unless you want Con Hổ to catch me mid-explanation."

"I'm not going any further until you tell us who you are," said Liên. "You can walk and talk at the same time, can't you?"

Freddie followed Liên's lead and stopped. She was surprised by her cousin's take-charge attitude, but in a good way.

Motorcycle Guy sighed. This wasn't a fight he could win. Finally, he whipped off his helmet and a mess of black hair tumbled out.

It was Duy.

CHAPTER 10

"Duy?!" Liên cried, surprised.

Freddie was a little less shocked by the reveal. She'd had an inkling that there was more to Duy than meets the eye when she spotted him getting berated by Nhất at the ceremony.

"Yes, hi, it's me." His thick, dark hair was messier than usual—strands were plastered to his sweaty forehead and his loose ponytail was frayed and askew.

"Wait." Liên shook her head, her thoughts playing catch up with the new facts. "Nhất is your dad. Your dad is the enemy! Which means *you're* the—"

"No. I'm not." Duy frowned.

There was a flash of anger in his eyes, the same kind

of fury Freddie saw in Nhất when he'd slammed his fist down on Ông Ngoại's desk. Like father, like son. Duy turned his attention back to the bike, grunting as he pushed it forward.

"What's your plan then? Where are we going exactly?" asked Freddie. "To another town? Back to Vỏ Rùa Làng? Our parents are probably freaking out that they can't find us."

Duy dug into his pocket and flipped open a small handheld compass. "'Fraid not. We can't be on the road. Not for a while. Con Hổ will be looking for you. They'll all be looking for you."

"*They?*" asked Liên. "You mean as in *your dad*?"

Duy kept his steely gaze ahead of him. "Yes. Exactly. And all his hired goons." He had a cool, even way of speaking, even if he was delivering terrifying news.

"You have to let us call our family at least," Freddie said.

"Absolutely not. They're monitoring everything. If they catch us out here, we're dead. We need to hide and lay low until I can think of something. It's our only chance."

Freddie felt as though her brain would ooze out of her ears at any second. Although she wasn't sure if Duy could be trusted, she was happy not to have to make a decision for a change, even if she wasn't entirely convinced that wandering aimlessly in a dense jungle was a safer option. What else were she and Liên supposed to do? They had no idea where they were.

They continued on, trudging past gleaming waterfalls, finding narrow footpaths through the brush, and pushing the small motorbike through shallow streams. It wasn't easy navigating a motorbike through unpaved jungle, but whenever Freddie imagined that Con Hổ was right behind them, it gave her the extra bit of energy to push through. Even Liên managed to keep up, occasionally using her scarf to wipe the sweat from the back of her neck.

Every now and then, Duy would suddenly stop to listen for something. Whenever he froze, the girls followed like a game of red light, green light. Each time, Freddie strained to hear whatever it was that made Duy go on alert, but she heard only the occasional birdcall in the distance. There was one bird in particular that sounded like it was practically screaming. Freddie had never heard a bird like that before; it made a high-pitched wail that was unsettling at first. Every time the bird screeched, Liên would start to laugh, which made Freddie laugh, which made Duy shush them to be quiet. The screaming bird instantly became Freddie's favorite. She even tried to mimic it by whistling back.

"That's a pretty good impression," said Liên. "Sounds exactly like it."

"Great. Maybe I'll get a job as a professional exotic bird caller if we ever get out of here," said Freddie. She checked on her eye. It was still tender to the touch from when the durian beaned her. "Hey, how's my shiner?"

Liên couldn't fight a smile. "Still there."

"That bad?"

"You don't want to know."

The farther they got, the thicker the humid air felt like it was choking them. Freddie stopped trying to wipe the sweat that was streaming down the back of her shirt. It seemed pointless after a while. And even though Duy kept referring to his compass, the worried look on his face didn't instill much confidence that he knew exactly what he was doing or where he was going.

Still, they kept walking.

"I've got a few thoughts," Freddie said, feeling confident that no man, let alone a tiger man, could hear their conversation now.

"Sure," said Duy. His tone was almost annoyed at the hassle of having to speak. "I'll take questions from the class now."

"How about starting with why your dad is trying to kill us?"

"My dad isn't trying to kill you. It's not even about you," said Duy. "He's after the crossbow."

"Are you talking about the An Dương Vương legend?" said Liên, with a snort-laugh. "You can't be serious. A magical crossbow?"

But Duy wasn't laughing. His face grew grim. Duy didn't seem like the kidding-around type. "It's real. Let's just get that part out of the way. If either of you had any doubt that it might be a made up thing from a fairy tale, you need to adjust your mindset now. The crossbow is very real and it's very dangerous. I don't have to tell you what it would be like if it got in the hands of some very bad dudes."

"*Sooo*, like your dad?" Liên didn't even try to mask her accusatory tone.

Duy's jaw clenched. "Yes, like my dad. Why do you think he's been funding your ông ngoại's research all these years? He's obsessed with finding the crossbow—always has been. He's moved us all over the country trying to track down any lead. It's all he's ever talked about. He's kind of like your ông ngoại in that wa—"

"Don't," said Freddie. "Your dad is *nothing* like Ông Ngoại."

Duy raised his hand. "I'm sorry. I didn't mean it like that. I just meant that I can't think of two other souls in this universe that share a very specific, mutual respect and devotion to finding that old relic. Why else would my dad throw our entire family's fortune at it? You think people like Con Hổ come cheap?"

"Who is that guy anyway?" asked Freddie. "He's like the Hulk or something. He's indestructible. He can't be stopped."

"Con Hổ is my dad's favorite hired muscle. Been with him since the beginning. Some of my earliest memories are of him coming to the house visiting my dad for these private meetings, but I still don't even know his real name. He's kept your ông ngoại under surveillance for years."

"That must be why he was at the train station when you arrived, Freddie!" Liên said. "And at the market."

"I *told* you there was something off about that guy."

"This is what I mean," Duy said. "My dad has eyes everywhere. You two are lucky to be alive. Seriously. If you see him again—and I hope you don't—you run the other way and don't look back, you hear me?"

"So, basically what we've always done," Freddie chimed in sarcastically. "Will do."

"He almost nailed us back there." Liên pointed to where the side mirror should have been.

"Con Hổ didn't miss his shot. He was aiming for the bike. If he wanted us dead, we would be," said Duy. "But you two are too valuable alive. You're collateral now, don't you get it? If your ông ngoại doesn't lead my dad to the crossbow—"

"Ông Ngoại!" Freddie got so caught up in the Nhất and Con Hổ of it all that she forgot to ask about the state of her grandfather. She anxiously spun Ông Ngoại's bracelet on her wrist. It seemed so strange to think that not too long ago Ông Ngoại was sharing the memory of Freddie sneaking off with this very same bracelet. "Is he okay? Is he hurt?"

"He's fine. For now. Your grandpa is very comfortable up in the luxury car with my dad at the front of the caravan. My dad has a whole team headed to Đà Nẵng," said Duy. "You two got stuck with Con Hổ at the very back of the line."

"I don't get it," Liên said. "How does Ông Ngoại fit

into all this? I mean, I get that he and your dad had some kind of business arrangement, but if they were partners trying to find the crossbow for so long . . . why is this all happening now?"

"You want to know what I think?" asked Duy. "I think your grandfather has either just learned where the crossbow is or he's come very close."

Freddie's eyes lit up. "So *that's* why he's suddenly retiring. He's scared that someone is actually going to find it. Kind of like a be-careful-what-you-wish-for sorta thing."

Duy nodded. "I couldn't stop them from taking your grandfather, but I did manage to get this . . ."

Carefully, Duy pulled out something that had been tucked into the back of his pants—a small leather-bound book.

"Ông Ngoại's diary!" Freddie exclaimed.

"Yes," Duy said. "I was able to get to it before my dad did. Maybe this will help us figure out where exactly in Đà Nẵng your grandfather is leading them to."

Freddie snatched the book from Duy's hands. She flipped through the pages and frowned. Of course everything was written in Vietnamese. Even though she didn't know Duy very well, she couldn't help but feel embarrassed that she couldn't read it.

"It's a good thing we found each other," Duy said. "Because I'm sure you two can fill in the gaps for me. From what I've read so far, your grandfather never specifically calls out where the crossbow is."

Liên couldn't hold back the biggest question any longer. "Why should we trust you?"

"Why don't we start with the fact that I saved you from Con Hổ—twice? Or the fact that I could've handed this diary over to my dad from the beginning?" said Duy, a twinge of annoyance in his voice. Freddie couldn't help but notice that flicker of Duy's father's specific brand of anger again. He sighed, pulling back. "Listen, I know this doesn't look great, but I swear to you: I'm not my dad."

Freddie looked to Duy, and their eyes met. It was the first time Duy returned their gaze directly. The anger in his eyes now looked more like a desperate plea. She searched for some sign that she could trust him with their most important possession—the only thing that could give them a fighting chance. Freddie started to hand the journal back. Duy's hand grasped the book, but Freddie didn't let go. Not yet.

"We just want our ông ngoại back." Freddie released

her grip on the diary. "Your dad and Con Hổ have a head start. But maybe we can beat them to it."

"I agree," said Duy. "But we're not going anywhere until I can fix this bike."

"Great. I'm sure we're bound to bump into a friendly gibbon running a mechanic shop out here," said Liên, collapsing against a rock. "I need a break and some water"

Duy tossed his packback to the ground. "Check in here. I grabbed whatever I could before I took off after you guys."

Freddie laid out the items one by one. There wasn't much. Two bottles of soda—some kind of melon cream flavor—and a small bundle wrapped in green banana leaves and tied with red strings. Then she plucked a bag containing what looked like two round, orange-sized buns.

"Bánh cam!" Freddie continued rifling through the goodies. "We got two balls of sesame buns, some Fanta. What about this?" She held up the round bundle.

Liên fist pumped. "Chả lụa! Vietnamese sausage." Duy used his knife to slice off a disk of soft, beige pork roll and handed it to Liên, then another for Freddie.

Freddie chewed slowly, savoring each bite. She bit

down on a piece of peppercorn, relishing its spark of spice. Before she knew it, she'd already swallowed it whole. Duy cut another slice for everyone.

Liên resumed rifling through the bag while looking at Duy. "What else do we have in here? Did you pack anything useful, like a hotel room?"

"Afraid I'm fresh out of those," said Duy, popping open the bike seat. "Didn't think we'd be stranded in the middle of nowhere. But I do have a flashlight, the machete, my switchblade, and a lighter."

"So what *was* your plan exactly?" Liên asked, swatting at mosquitos. "Your dad and his band of merry men are the ones that forced us into the jungle! And now we have barely any food and only a couple bottles of soda. We're doomed!" It wasn't like Liên to get so snappy, but she was out of her element. Freddie was used to pivoting when she needed to, but improvisation didn't come easy to Liên. Freddie wasn't even sure if Liên had stepped foot outside Vỏ Rùa Làng before.

"No one is doomed," Duy said. "We're going to Đà Nẵng, remember?"

"By *walking*?"

"You have a better idea?"

All this bickering wasn't making things easier for

Freddie to digest everything that had happened to them up until now. Of course she wanted a clear plan as badly as Liên did, but there had to be a better way to get what they all wanted.

"Okay, *children*, relax." Freddie chided. "Let me think!"

She surveyed the area, trying to find something—*anything*—that could be promising. Up on an overlook, Freddie spotted something that looked like it could be a decently sized cave. They'd have to climb to get there, but it didn't look too strenuous.

"There!" she pointed. "Why don't we regroup at that cave? It would give us some cover so we could rest."

Liên and Duy nodded in agreement though it was obvious there was still static between them. They all stood around in awkward silence, waiting to see who would make the first move. It was bigger, darker, and deeper than Freddie had anticipated.

Duy cracked his neck and shook his arms, as if wiggling the nerves out. "I'm going to check it out."

Is he . . . putting on a brave front? Freddie wondered. This was the first hint of vulnerability from the surly stranger. Duy grabbed a flashlight from the seat of the bike and climbed up the embankment to reach the cave.

"You don't have to go in there alone," said Freddie. "I'll go with you."

If Duy heard her, he didn't answer.

But as Duy disappeared into the cave, Freddie knew it was the last thing Duy wanted to do.

CHAPTER 11

Some time had passed and there was still no sign of Duy. "Should we have volunteered to go with him?" asked Freddie.

"No way. If he's going to try and act all macho and not ask for our help, I'm not offering it up to him." Liên looked to the sky at the exact same thing Freddie was looking at. It was getting dark now, and the moon was peeking out. It had been a long day. "Freddie, why are we even trusting this kid? He's the son of the enemy!"

"What are we supposed to do, ditch him when he's trying to find us shelter—after he saved us? I don't think karma would look too kindly on us." Freddie reasoned. "Besides, it's not like we know how to navigate our way through this jungle. We don't even know where we are!"

"Then it doesn't matter if we go on without him! I say we find a way out of this jungle and get back home . . . together."

It didn't feel right to completely abandon the one person who had saved them from Con Hổ. Twice. As much as she wanted to side with Liên, Freddie had to go with her gut. "Look, it's getting dark and I think we need all the help we can get right now, Liên."

"So you're saying you trust him more than you trust me?"

"What? No! Of course not." Freddie knew she had to choose her next words carefully.

The fact was, Freddie *did* trust Duy in this situation. It was a matter of survival, and somehow, Freddie knew they had a better chance of doing that if they stuck together. And besides, it wasn't that Freddie *didn't* trust Liên. It was simply . . . a complicated situation.

"I'm just saying that he seems to know what he's doing. How much jungle knowledge do you have, Liên? I don't have any problem admitting that I don't have any."

Liên turned her chin up toward the cave. "Keep an eye on that entrance. I'll bet you my college fund that that boy will come running out any second."

Sure enough, there was a scream, followed by Duy racing out of the cave stumbling over himself as he slid down the embankment's slope. Liên winked at Freddie as if to say *Told you so.*

"New plan." He was cradling his left arm. "There's definitely something in there. Tell me you heard that." He stared up at the cave as if waiting for something to emerge.

"The only thing we heard was a yelp of terror, and that came from you," said Liên.

"What'd you do with the flashlight?" asked Freddie. "What happened in there?"

Duy gulped some air, catching his breath. He began pacing. "I think someone was living in that cave. There was definitely some kind of a . . . a campsite or something. I didn't get too good a look. I saw something moving. And then I heard a squeal. I can't believe you didn't hear it. So then I started running, and then I tripped on some stupid—Ow!" Duy had raised his arms, wincing.

"Okay, seriously," said Freddie, watching Duy keep his arm close to his chest. "What is going on with your arm?"

"It's nothing," he said. "I tripped and fell and landed on it weird."

"Can I look at it?"

"Not like I can stop you."

As slowly as she could, Freddie rolled up Duy's sleeve and held back a gag. A nasty bump had already formed on his forearm. And it would only get worse. Freddie was no stranger to this, given how many spills she'd taken at skateparks.

"It might be broken." She swallowed after getting those words out. "We need to get you to a hospital."

Duy tugged his sleeve back down. "We're only a few hours from Đà Nẵng . . ."

"On bike!" shouted Liên. Her frustration was frothing to a boil. "We're a few hours away on a motorcycle. Not to mention, we don't even have *that* right now!"

"Yeah . . . I'm still working on that," Duy said.

"Well, if we have any hope of getting the bike fixed and out of this jungle," said Freddie, picking up Duy's machete, "then that arm is going to need something a little more permanent to hold it in place. I'll be back soon."

"Where are you going? I'm coming with you," said Liên.

"I'm not going far." Freddie knew Liên wanted to go too, but Freddie couldn't live with herself if another person got hurt because of her. "Stay with Duy. I don't think we can afford another broken bone."

"For the record, I really don't think it's a good idea for us to separate in a jungle!" yelled Liên.

The hazy glow of the moon provided more than enough light. It didn't take long for Freddie to find acluster of bamboo. Perfect. Once she eyed a stalk that she thought might work, she gave it a few good whacks with the machete. She heard a tiny shriek. Something fluttered out of the bamboo. Then another. Then another. Now it was Freddie's turn to shriek.

Liên came running. "What? What is it? Are you okay?"

Freddie's hand was still clutching her heart. She swallowed then pointed to the bamboo stalk she managed to cleave. Liên inched her way to the bamboo, then peered inside.

"Baby bats. You woke up some baby bats." Liên laughed. She helped Freddie to her feet and brought her over to the bamboo stalk. Nestled inside were two furry bat babies, still sleeping. "You have to admit they're cute."

"No one told me bats sleep in bamboo," said Freddie, her heart still pounding. "Like you wouldn't have freaked out if a bat came flying at you!"

"Hey, we're in the jungle now. Anything's possible." Liên shrugged. "Care to clue me in as to why you're chopping bamboo?"

Right. Duy's arm. "I have an idea," she said.

She scooped up the piece of bamboo she hacked off and ran back to camp with Liên behind her. Freddie cut a few strips from the bottom of her áo dài. Then she sliced the piece of bamboo straight down the middle length-wise. She took one half of the bamboo and slid it under Duy's arm. Using the fabric strips, she tied the bamboo around his shoulder. Now it was secure. She felt a tiny bubble of pride at what she'd accomplished.

"There you go," Freddie said, rather proud of herself. "Instant sling! Not sure how long it'll last, but it might make you feel better for now."

Duy looked it over. "It fits. How'd you come up with that?"

"My friend Nisa took a pretty bad spill down at Burnside once. I remember the nurses saying that if it were to happen again that we should find a way to keep the arm as stiff as possible. I figured bamboo was as sturdy as it gets and, hey, we're surrounded by a lot of it."

"I guess we were due for a bit of luck," said Liên.

And then it happened. Large, dark, dots pelted the ground.

Rain. A lot of it. And it was coming down hard.

Liên let the rain pour all around her. "*Good* luck. I meant we're due for a bit of *good* luck."

CHAPTER 12

"This is stupid. I'm going in," said Liên, stomping up toward the cave.

"Liên, no!" Freddie tugged at her elbow. If something in there scared off Duy enough for him to stumble and fracture bone, for sure Liên wouldn't be able to handle it. "You're not running into a cave all by yourself. If anyone is going, it's me."

Liên yanked her arm away. "Are you going to start telling me I can't go to the market by myself either?"

"Okay, going to pick up a bag of tamarind and going into a creepy cave with someone living in it aren't the same thing!" Freddie knew Liên could be stubborn, but clearly the jungle was messing with the logic portion of her brain.

"Why does it have to be *you*?" Liên asked.

"Because . . ." Freddie scrambled to find the words to explain that she couldn't bear to see her cousin get hurt. She grabbed a handful of twigs and leaves and shoved them in her pockets—anything that hadn't gotten wet from the rain yet. "Just . . . *because*, okay?" She turned to Duy. "*Really* wish you hadn't dropped that flashlight. Where's that lighter?"

"Freddie. No. No way." Duy was at his feet, blocking her path. "There's something in there. I'm telling you!"

Freddie pushed past him, snatching the lighter from Duy's hands. "You can't fix a bike in the rain. If you're right about someone living in that cave, maybe there's something useful for us inside. And the sooner you get that bike up and running, the sooner we can get out of this jungle. I'm getting us a roof." Armed with Duy's lighter and the machete, Freddie stomped her way to the cave.

She scrambled up the slope to the cave's entrance. A cool breeze swept in, drying the sweat on her forearms. The ledge provided a perfect top view of the jungle; it was pretty amazing not to see another car, person, or building. Freddie had never been camping before, at least not outside her own backyard, but she was starting to understand why people liked it so much. The stars were out and at their brightest. Not a single sound beyond rustling leaves. This was her first time experiencing nature in its rawest form.

Right, the cave, she thought, her attention snapping back to the task at hand. She looked into the dark abyss that was the cave's mouth, Duy's lighter shaking in her hand and the machete trembling at her side. She had a plan to lure out whatever was in there. Or at least half of a plan. Maybe half of a half of a plan.

She wiped the lighter on her thigh, hoping to dry it off as best she could. The only way her plan would work was if the lighter lit right away. If not, she was in serious trouble. Freddie stepped one foot in, then the other until all she could see was complete darkness. The smell of earth and wet dirt surrounded her. The only thing she could hear was the faint sound of trickling water. She groped in the dark a bit, feeling her way around the rocks. The plan was to be stealthy first—in and out without any confrontation. That would be ideal.

Freddie fought to keep her panic at bay. She hoped her eyes would adjust enough so that she could scan the floor for the flashlight. Her fingers grasped at the dirt. Where was it? She inched a few more paces in. The rocks between her shoes crunched. Every so often, she turned back to the mouth of the cave to reorient herself. The moonlight was growing fainter.

Suddenly she heard something. A shuffling. She froze in place, listening for more. When it was quiet again, Freddie set down the machete and felt around for rocks, making a circle with them before emptying her pockets with the dried twigs and leaves. Her fire pit was complete. There was a decent amount of kindling. It'd have to do.

Freddie clicked open the lighter when she heard it. At first, she thought it was her mind playing tricks on her. She heard something. A kind of soft puffing. Huffing, maybe? She didn't want to raise the lighter in the direction of the noise. Maybe it was like a tyrannosaurus rex—if she didn't move, it wouldn't see her.

That's when she found what she'd been searching for. The flashlight! Freddie slowly reached for it.

But the grunts and huffs were getting louder. Freddie clicked on the flashlight and aimed its beam toward the back of the cave. Duy was right: there were definitely signs that someone had been living in the cave, or at least taking shelter here. A fisherman or maybe a hunter, perhaps?

Then, from the shadows, Freddie spotted them— the very eyes that had scared Duy out of the cave. It was . . .

A pig.

No, not a pig. This wasn't a cute pink farm animal frolicking in the mud. This beast was feral. Enormous, with bristly, twisted hair with two nasty-looking tusks jutting from its snarled lips. A wild boar. And it looked like she was a mother, seeing as there were three spotted baby boars huddled next to her.

Freddie didn't know much about wild boars, but she did know that animals—especially mothers—were usually very protective of their children. And the grunts didn't sound happy. She kept the light trained on the mom. Maybe if Freddie made slow movements, she wouldn't make the mom mad.

"Easy, girl," Freddie whispered as calmly as she could muster, more for her own reassurance than for the boar's. With her free hand, Freddie clicked on the lighter. Nothing.

An angry snort. A warning.

Click. Nothing.

A high-pitched squeal bounced off the cave walls. The boar took a few cautious steps forward. Mama wanted Freddie out of that cave.

Freddie needed to make a decision. She could either keep trying with the lighter or grab the machete and make a run for it. The boar was still far enough away that Freddie felt confident she could make it out of the cave in one piece.

No. Freddie couldn't give up. She, Liên, and Duy needed shelter. They needed to get out of the rain. They needed sleep. They needed to fix the bike. They needed the cave, and Freddie was taking it.

Click.

Fire!

Freddie lowered the lighter to the pile of twigs. A few puffs of smoke billowed from the kindling, but it wasn't enough. For her plan to work, the fire needed to generate more smoke—lots more smoke.

Another squeal. A squeal that Freddie felt in her toes. Time to go.

Freddie turned and sprinted as fast as she could toward the entrance. Mama boar was right behind her,

Freddie could feel it. She pumped her arms and pleaded with her legs to move faster. She remembered her gym teacher telling her to breathe through her nose and exhale through her mouth. Yeah, right. That technique didn't seem to make her run any faster.

Freddie's toe caught on something—a root or a jutting rock—that sent her crashing to the ground and cut her thigh on the way down. Then she felt a sharp, stinging jab in her side. Furious snorting, the distinct smell of earth and animal. Mama Boar had headbutted her! Freddie hoped the tusks didn't find their way into her gut. Being skewered in the middle of the jungle was not the way she wanted to go.

The taste of blood and dirt filled Freddie's mouth. She must have bit her tongue. She spat. There was no time to worry about that now. *Get up*, Freddie screamed in her head. *Get up and run! Move!*

Even though she couldn't see the boar, Freddie could sense that the boar was coming back again. For a split second, Freddie's saw a glimpse of Con Hổ bracing himself as Duy sped toward him on the motorcycle, which gave her an idea. Freddie would get only one shot at this. She had to make it count . . . or else. Freddie braced herself as the boar bolted at her.

Come on, Freddie thought, forcing herself to keep her eyes open. *Just a little closer . . .*

And then, at the last second before impact, Freddie swung the flashlight with all her might. A direct hit! The instrument connected and the boar skittered across the cave floor, stumbling backward, stunned. Freddie wasn't sticking around to see what would happen next. Her thigh burned, but the cave's mouth was right there. She was free! As Freddie spilled out into the cool, night air, she didn't dare look behind her. Freddie scrambled up the side of the cave, slipping on the rain-slicked rocks. At the top, she found a tree, bent by wind, and managed to climb up its trunk.

The rain pelted her face, but at least Freddie could finally breathe, her lungs searing as they filled with air. Her shaking fingers dug into the bark of the tree, the old bracelet dangling on her wrist. How it managed to stay fastened through that debacle was a mystery.

When Freddie built up the courage to look down, she wasn't surprised to see the mama boar circling the tree. The boar squealed an ear-piercing warning for Freddie to stay away from her babies. Fair enough. Soon, the fire's smoke would do the rest of the work.

That is, if it didn't get snuffed out during the chase.

Eventually, Mama gave up. As fierce as she was, hooves were no match for a slippery tree trunk. Freddie kept her eyes trained on Mama as the boar retreated to her home.

That's right, thought Freddie. *Go home. Get your kiddos. Keep them safe.*

All there was left to do was to wait.

The minutes dragged on. Freddie shivered as the rain continued to pour. She kept her eyes on the cave, reminding herself to blink. Now that she wasn't in any immediate danger, the wave of feelings started to come back. Her side throbbed. No broken bones, she didn't think, but there was definitely going to be a bruise. She spat some more blood as she found a better grip on the tree. Her fingers felt like icicles, but she had to hold out a little longer.

Then she saw it. A wispy trail of smoke swirled from the cave. Exactly what she was hoping for. The little brown-and-white spotted piglets came out, followed by their big ol' huffy mama. Freddie took a moment for herself. She made this happen.

Once Freddie felt confident that mama boar and her babies were long gone, she climbed down from the safety of the tree and limped back to the ledge where the mouth of the cave was.

"Are you okay?" asked Liên, calling up. "I was about ready to come in after you!"

"I'll be better once we get by that fire," said Freddie, shouldering the backpack. "Come on. Let's get out of this rain."

CHAPTER 13

Freddie doused the fire she'd worked so hard to light. Liên had the idea to rebuild the fire toward the back of the cave because the smoke didn't seem to be as bad there; it floated to the roof of the cave and out the entrance. The cave wasn't exactly warm, but at least they were dry.

By some miracle, Freddie and Liên managed to move the motorbike inside, and Duy went to work assessing the damage. Meanwhile, Freddie and Liên searched the cave for any supplies that could be useful. Whoever had been there didn't leave much behind. There was a makeshift table and, on top of it, a half-finished game of chess, though some pieces had fallen onto the ground.

Two upturned milk crates had been used as chairs. Some old fishing poles. A metal wash bin with half a bottle of dish soap and an old rag. Two sleeping bags were splayed out, even if they were more than a bit dusty. But there was no first aid kit, no food, and no water, apart from the rain.

The comforting glow of the flickering flames was a welcomed treat. Now, if only there was a plate of spaghetti drenched in marinara with giant meatballs and melted, shaved parmesan to go with it. Freddie shook the image from her head. What was the point of dreaming of food? She needed to figure out how to get out of this mess.

Freddie walked over to Duy who was squatting next to the bike. "We checked the hunter's supplies," she said. "Fresh out of new motorcycles, which means it's all up to you, bud."

Duy ran a hand through his hair, pushing the strands out of his face. "Any chance they left behind a new set of brake cables?"

"Maybe. If I had any idea what a brake cable was."

Duy scooted over so Freddie could get a better look, even though she didn't know exactly what she was supposed to be looking at. "When we took that spill back there, the bike's brake cable snapped. So when I squeeze this rear brake lever"—he gripped the handlebar and pointed to the back of the bike—"it's supposed to move this cable right here to activate the brakes. But the cable is toast."

"Well, I don't think there's a spare one of those around here," she said, scanning the room. Suddenly, an idea began to form in her head. "But what if we used something else? What if we used this?" She snatched up a fishing pole and brought it over. "Couldn't you use a fishing line to make, like, a temporary cable?"

Duy considered it for a moment, and for the first time, he let a smile slip. "You know what . . . that just might work."

Freddie unraveled the line and began weaving them together—kind of like the boondoggles she made at summer camp. Before she knew it, she held a fairly solid braid of fishing line in her hands. Freddie felt a bubble of pride in her chest. She turned to tell Liên, but Liên wasn't paying attention. She was on the other side of the cave, doing that strange dance again. Freddie watched as Liên unwrapped the checkered scarf from her neck and practiced a series of martial art techniques by herself, spinning and high-kicking in sharp, deliberate movements. The scarf, now frayed and stained with mud, would flutter around her as she continued to dance around in some kind of premeditated formation. From what Freddie could see, Liên wasn't exactly graceful, but she seemed determined to keep at it.

Freddie waited for Liên to finish, or at least to acknowledge that she was there. But Liên kept at her routine, as if Freddie were invisible. Finally, Freddie stepped in front of Liên, interrupting her movement. "Hello? I'm standing here trying to tell you something."

"Sorry," said Liên, tucking a strand of hair behind her ear. There was an iciness to her tone. "I was practicing."

"Yeah, I got that." Freddie swallowed her own annoyance. "I just came over to tell you that I think we found a way to fix the bike. We may have a way out of this jungle!"

Liên offered a half nod and a forced smile. "Great. Good for you guys." Then she turned and went back to her routine.

Freddie was left stunned. Feeling awkward, and perhaps a little sad, she turned and marched back to Duy, who was already making good work with the fishing line. "I don't know what her deal is."

"Well, I can't imagine being lost in a remote jungle is helping to improve her mood," said Duy, carefully threading the braided line through the bike. "Can you hold the hook here?"

Freddie held the fishing hook in place as instructed. "I never thought alienating my favorite cousin was going to be on my highlight reel for this summer vacation."

"You probably didn't imagine getting kidnapped and chasing down a mythical crossbow was on your agenda either," said Duy with a half smile. After a moment, he continued, "Besides all the kidnapping and being shot at . . . how are you enjoying your time back home?"

"Are you trying to get to know me?" Freddie asked, returning her own half smile.

"Why not? We've got time to kill."

Freddie looked over at Liên, who was still practicing her Bà Trà. It wasn't like Liên was speaking with her at the moment.

"Being back here, it's like . . . it's like walking through a fog or a hologram or something. Like it's something that's right in front of me, but I can't quite grab a hold of it. All these memories are starting to come back, but not as quickly as I'd want, you know? It's taking a lot of time to fill in the holes. And don't even get me started about the language."

"Oh?" Duy said, slightly surprised. "I've heard you speak. You're fine."

"And you're a liar." Freddie laughed. She stared out the cave entrance. The stars weren't out, but the rain was starting to let up a bit. "The funny thing is, I used to be fluent. But my mom and I must have stopped speaking Vietnamese when we moved to the US. She wanted to practice her English and I didn't see the point in speaking Vietnamese when I didn't have to—no one on TV spoke it. No one at school did. None of my friends. So eventually . . . it started slipping away. And now I come back here after all this time, and I can barely talk to my own family."

"It'll come back to you," said Duy. "Vietnamese is a very—"

"Literal language. I know, I know."

Duy sat back and cracked his neck. "From what I saw at the ceremony, your family didn't seem to care if you spoke perfect Vietnamese or not. You were laughing a lot. They were laughing a lot. If you wanna trade families, you let me know."

Freddie felt a twinge of guilt. Here she was

complaining about family when Duy had the most complicated family of all. She let the moment sit, wondering how to bring up Nhất.

Finally, she said, "Your dad seems pretty . . . complicated."

"That's one way to put it. I wouldn't say he's a very happy person," Duy crouched back down, careful to not knock his slinged arm, and went back to work. "But from what I've pieced together, he got it pretty bad from my ông nội, and I'm sure my ông nội got it from his dad. Maybe there was a time when my dad wasn't so angry, but it only seems to be getting worse. I don't know how to describe it. He's just mad. All. The. Time.

"And whenever he thought he had a lead on the crossbow and it didn't pan out, or if he thought your ông ngoại was close to discovering a new location and it turned out to be a dead end . . . those were the worst times."

Freddie felt a pit in her stomach. She swallowed but said nothing. She could see the pain in Duy's eyes, even though he tried hard to hide his gaze by focusing only on the task at hand.

"Your ông ngoại. He made it his life's work to find this thing, this crossbow. My dad did too. But with your ông ngoại, it was his passion. He enjoyed the journey, the thrill of the hunt. But my dad . . . it's only ever about the end result. This crossbow isn't something he's passionate about. It's his *obsession*. And I'm afraid it's gonna kill him one way or another."

Freddie's eyes started to burn and itch, as if the tears would break at any moment. How lucky she was to have a family that cared about her. "Do you actually think the crossbow is real?"

"Yes, I do," said Duy matter-of-factly. "We have to stop him, Freddie. He can't get his hands on it." Before Freddie could formulate her next thought, Duy stood up. "Finished. Give it a shot."

Freddie placed her hand on the handlebar and gave it a squeeze. The braided fishing line held, causing the brake to move with each squeeze. "I think we've got ourselves a working bike! I'd give you a high five, but, you know . . . your broken arm."

"I appreciate that."

Freddie cupped her hands around her mouth. "Liên! You hear that? We got the bike working!"

Liên flashed a thumbs-up. "When can we get out of here?"

"Soon. First thing tomorrow," said Duy. "We can

catch up to them in Đà Nẵng. But for now, we should try and sleep. Maybe we should do shifts? You know, just in case Con Hổ is out there, or there's another wild boar . . . or worse."

"Sure," Freddie said. "I'll—"

"*I'll* do the first shift," Liên interjected. "I mean . . . if that's okay with you?" The tartness in Liên's tone wasn't subtle.

Freddie shrugged. "If that's what you want. Wake me if you start to get tired."

Liên walked past Freddie and resumed her Bà Trà.

Freddie flipped the sleeping bags, getting the dust off. The bags were both in pretty good condition all things considered. She slipped into hers and Duy into his.

"I told you she's mad," whispered Freddie.

"She'll be fine," said Duy. "Just give her some space."

Freddie wasn't so sure this was a matter of space. Something else was wrong with Liên. But Freddie wasn't going to figure it out now. She closed her eyes and fell asleep before she could worry about her cousin a second more.

CHAPTER 14

Freddie awoke to something nudging her. She sprang up and reached for the machete that she'd placed next to her.

"Relax!" Liên raised her hands. "It's me! It's time for your shift."

Freddie waited for her heart rate to settle back down. She was certainly awake now. Then she remembered that Liên was still annoyed with her. Freddie sat up on her elbows. She supposed now was as good a time as any to bring it up with her cousin.

"Hey . . . Liên?" Freddie asked carefully. "Are we cool?"

Freddie climbed out of the bag, and then Liên slipped into it. "Yeah."

"I know you," Freddie said, "and that *yeah* doesn't sound real to me."

"I thought you knew me too," said Liên, shedding her glasses before rolling over.

"What's that supposed to mean?"

"Forget it," Liên said with a huff. "I just want to go to sleep, okay?"

Freddie stood there for a moment. "Yeah. Okay."

But the thing was, it wasn't okay. At least not for Freddie. If she had it her way, she'd force her cousin to stay up and confess what was really going on. But Freddie knew that Liên getting a good few hours of sleep was more important.

Freddie sucked in a breath and clenched her teeth. Her whole side felt like a piece of tenderized meat. That boar had gotten her good. She lifted her shirt, gently pressing her ribs. Another dark purplish bruise had formed overnight, right where the wild boar had nailed her. Freddie had taken her fair share of spills in skate park bowls, but she'd never limped away with a bruise like this.

She walked over to Duy's motorbike and popped open the seat compartment. There was a little soda and chả lụa left. She bit off some sausage and took a swig of the melon cream soda but made sure there was some left for Duy and Liên.

Freddie tested the brakes again (to her relief, they still worked), then made her way to the cave entrance. The rain had stopped. The moon was full. There was the familiar screeching cry of her favorite bird, but there were other strange noises she couldn't place: a throaty clacking; a twig snapping; leaves rustling; curious creatures shuffling around the outskirts of their camp. Unseen cicadas screamed ominously, as if warning the kids to get out of the jungle. Freddie couldn't shake the uneasy feeling that they were being watched.

After a while, she heard something peculiar, but it wasn't coming from the jungle—it was coming from behind her. Freddie rushed into the cave to find that the mystery noise was a whimper. It was Duy. He twisted and turned, drenched in a shivering sweat. Classic signs of a nightmare.

"Duy. Duy!" Freddie said, shaking him.

She pried open his eyelid and saw something strange: a glint of gold. It scared her. Duy kept kicking and bucking. She wondered if she should wake up Liên. Freddie tapped his cheek with the back of her hand. No response.

"Sorry in advance," she said, and then she slapped him a little harder.

Duy sat up, gasping for breath.

"Are you okay?" asked Freddie.

"Yeah. Well, except for this little thing with my arm here," said Duy. "But you already knew about that."

"I don't mean your arm," said Freddie. "You were having a nightmare, but, like, way scarier than a nightmare. I thought you were having a seizure or something."

"It's nothing. It happens from time to time," Duy said, but Freddie was unconvinced. "It's not a big deal. Sorry if I kept you up."

"Duy, it didn't *look* like nothing—"

"I'm *fine*." With that, Duy rolled over.

Freddie watched him for a little longer. The sleeping bag slowly rose and fell with each breath Duy took. She placed her hand on his forehead. He was still burning up.

He needs water, Freddie thought.

She grabbed the flashlight, an empty soda bottle, and Duy's compass, then headed outside. She'd only be a minute.

After sliding down the slope, Freddie made a point to orient herself using the compass. If she walked only in one direction, she'd be okay to find her way back. She picked a direction at random—east seemed as good as any—and if she got lost, she'd simply back track west.

Ten minutes into her walk, Freddie thought she heard a trickling of water. She broke into a jog, then a sprint, leaping over logs and pushing through thick brush. But when she got to an opening, all she saw was . . .

A white bird with a black stripe that looked like a mask was perched in a tree. When it saw her, it let out a familiar screech.

"Oh, it's you." Freddie had come face-to-face with her favorite bird. The feathers on its head stood up like a wild mohawk, reminding Freddie of Ông Ngoại's unruly mop of hair. "I think I'll call you Ông."

Freddie sat down, listening to Ông squawk away. She was tired and thirsty and suddenly felt an overwhelming crush of sadness wanting to see her family again. Her cousin hated her. Duy needed water. And here she was— alone in a jungle, her side aching from a run-in with a wild boar—trying to find the will to do anything at all. It was the last straw. Her dam was breaking.

"I need help, Ông." She put her face in her hands, fighting back tears. "I can't do this." A tear betrayed her, slipping from her eye and sliding down her cheek.

Ông fell silent, looking down at Freddie. No, not at Freddie—at her wrist. As Freddie wiped the tear away, she saw a soft golden glow radiating from her bracelet.

Freddie examined the bracelet, bemused. "What the . . ." She looked up to Ông, who slowly arced his head as if beckoning Freddie to look, too. Freddie matched the bird's eyeline.

Another soft golden glow came from off in the distance. Whatever it was, Freddie felt like it was connected to her bracelet somehow, and she needed to inspect it. Hey, it wasn't the strangest thing that had happened to her the past few days.

Freddie looked up at Ông. "Thank you," she said. Before she knew what she was doing, Freddie dusted herself off and sprinted after the golden light. She leapt over logs, vaulted over rocks, and ran through bushes. It was just beyond her reach.

Eventually, she found herself in front of a gorgeous waterfall spilling into a humble basin in a sort of secret oasis. And in the center of the basin was the source of the glow: a shell—an enormous turtle's shell. It was solid gold, half submerged in the water.

An ancient turtle stared at her. Deep wrinkles formed around his slow, blinking eyes. Freddie stared back.

Someone had to make the first move, but Freddie wasn't sure if what she was looking at was real. Was she delirious? Was this all in her head? Freddie kneeled down, splashing her face. This was no illusion, no trick of the mind.

Yep. The golden turtle was still there. It was huge—the size of her mom's king-size bed back home at least. A soft, warm light haloed his ancient shell. He blinked slowly at Freddie. Maybe he was expecting Freddie to break the ice.

"Hi," she began. "Um, I'm Freddie. Freddie Lỗ. Are you the turtle-god from the legend? I mean, you'd have to be—I can't think of too many stories that feature a golden turtle-god." If this was the same creature she thought it was, she wished he would say something already to end her rambling.

After a moment, the turtle-god said, "You . . . have the gift." His voice was slow, deep, and rumbling, and he took a breath between words. He blinked once. Twice.

"Me? A gift?" Freddie shook her head. Clearly, this turtle was from another plane of existence. "No, you're mistaken. I'm a nobody. I don't even know what I'm supposed to be doing."

"It must be returned," he continued, as if talking through her.

"Yes, the crossbow," said Freddie. "We're trying. But we have no idea what to do or where to go. Can . . . can you help us?"

The turtle's eyes glowed gold, and Freddie felt a chill Her stomach flip-flopped. She felt like she was falling somehow.

A moment later, Freddie realized she was no longer in the oasis. She was somewhere else entirely, as if inside a vision that was not her own. A vision of the turtle's making.

Sickly, dark clouds swirled in the sky. The ground was aflame. A shadowy figure stood before a massive army of shadows. In the figure's hands was the crossbow, brightly lit with a heavenly glow.

"Whoever controls the crossbow, controls the realm," came the turtle-god's voice. "The master of the crossbow alone can wield my magnificent power."

The dark figure raised the crossbow and pulled the trigger. A spray of golden light shot forth from the divine weapon. Its aim was true, piercing the hearts of the shadow soldiers. Most fell instantly. Some tried to flee only to be caught by an arrow to the back. Others begged for forgiveness or for their mothers, but their pleas were ignored. Hundreds of shadows turned to ashes that were swept away by a blistering wind. But the piercing, unrelenting screams of its victims echoed on.

Freddie gasped, throwing herself backward. She snapped out of the vision and was back at the waterfall.

"Okay, okay. I get it. But that's what I'm trying to tell you. I'm trying to find the crossbow as fast as I can, and I need help."

"It must . . . be returned . . . by the one who first received the gift."

Freddie thought for a moment. According to the legend, that would be King An Dương . . . but he was long gone.

"You mean the king?" said Freddie. "But the king died like thousands of years ago!"

"His blood lives on," said the turtle-god.

"What does that even *mean?*" asked Freddie, genuinely confused.

"Go . . . to Đà Nẵng," the turtle-god continued. "Return it . . . to me. You . . . have the gift."

"You keep saying that, but I'm not special. I'm just a kid lost in the jungle, and my cousin and my friend need help, and I'm *trying*," pleaded Freddie. "If you could just give me a little hint for where the crossbow is . . ."

"You . . . have the gift . . ." The golden turtle closed its sleepy eyes, and then it submerged into the oasis. It was gone.

Once again, Freddie was alone. She sat there for a moment, reflecting on what had just happened.

"Thanks . . . I guess," she said finally.

Freddie filled the bottle with rainwater collected from the waterfall and raced back to the cave. She had to tell Duy and Liên what she'd seen—that was, if they'd even believe her. Liên wouldn't, probably. But Duy might. He actually believed in this crossbow mumbo jumbo. Although Freddie had to admit . . . she was starting to buy into it too after what she'd just been through. But if what she's experienced *was* real, then that meant that they were on the right track. They had to get to Đà Nẵng. That was priority number one.

But when Freddie got back to the cave, she felt something was off. Seriously off.

She stepped inside, straining to listen, but couldn't hear a sound. The hairs on her arms raised.

"Liên? Duy?"

"Freddie!" came Liên's voice. "Don't come in here. Con Hổ!"

Freddie's heart thundered. She disobeyed and picked up her pace. "Where? Where is he?"

"No," Duy said. "Not him."

Freddie stopped. There, standing in right in front of her, was a real tiger.

CHAPTER 15

Duy was at one end of the cave, nearest to the motorcycle. Liên was at the other side, alone. And Freddie had come up behind the tiger. It was in the middle of their triangle.

The tiger was circling, slowly pacing, its piercing yellow eyes always trained on one of them. Its tail stood straight out and was stiff, like it was prepared to pounce at any second. The tiger was thin, probably hungry. Not a great sign.

"E—either of you have experience dealing with wild tigers?" Freddie forced herself to measure her breath to not sound completely freaked out.

"I didn't think tigers were even around here anymore," said Duy. "They're nearly extinct in Vietnam."

Freddie tried not to move. "Guess we're just that lucky, huh?"

The tiger turned to Freddie when she spoke. A low growl grumbled from its throat.

"It turns whenever someone makes noise," said Liên. On cue, the tiger spun around to Liên.

"Hey! Hey!" shouted Freddie. She wasn't about to let her cousin be the bait. The tiger circled again.

"The machete is over there. I'm gonna make a run for it," said Liên. "Someone grab that machete as soon as it comes for me." The tiger turned its massive head to Liên.

Duy remained frozen in place. "Liên. No. Don't."

"No! Don't be dumb," hissed Freddie. If they survived this, she was going to kill Liên.

"I can do this," Liên sucked in a breath. "I'm gonna do it. Get ready."

Panic rose in Freddie's throat. "Liên. Please."

"I'm doing this." Liên broke out into a sprint.

It felt like time slowed down to Freddie—that everything was in slow motion.

The tiger took the bait. It started for Liên.

Freddie tried to scream but the fear caught in her throat. She couldn't save her cousin.

Suddenly, Freddie saw a blinding flash of light. Then she heard a growl, but not from the tiger—from the motorbike, followed by the piercing cry of the bike's horn. Duy threw the bike into gear and drove straight for the tiger.

The tiger turned and sprinted past Freddie, nearly knocking her to the ground. He took a giant leap out of the cave entrance and disappeared. Duy slammed on the brakes. Guess they were working after all.

Liên was up against the cave wall, drenched in sweat. Her glasses dangled from her ear.

Freddie stomped over to her, shaking. "That was . . . incredibly stupid, Liên. You're supposed to be the smart one." Freddie didn't try to hide the fury and frustration in her tone.

Liên got right up in Freddie's face. "*Someone* had to do something! It's *your* fault this happened in the first place! You were supposed to be keeping watch!"

Duy glared at Liên from the motorcycle. "And you could have gotten yourself killed."

"I don't need you to chime in," said Liên. "For all I know, you're still with *them*."

"Seriously?" Duy threw up his hands. "We're doing this again?"

"Guys, guys!" Freddie forced herself to take a breath. She couldn't stand the bickering anymore. She knew that if she didn't do something, they were going to crumble. She had to keep them together, no matter what. "We're all hungry and miserable. I get it. But the way you two are going at each other, I'd rather take my chances with the tiger."

Duy turned the key, killing the engine. Liên stomped toward the cave's entrance.

"Where are you going?" asked Freddie, spinning Liên around by her shoulders. Her cheeks flushed and her jaw clenched. "You really think it's a good idea to be throwing a tantrum in the jungle? You've been acting weird ever since we got here. This isn't like you, and you know it."

"What do you know about me, Freddie? Huh?" Liên snapped. "You and everyone else in the family still think I'm this frail little bookworm who can't be trusted to do anything by herself. I can't even go to the market by myself without having a chaperone. You're not my babysitter. You think I'm weak."

"That's . . . that's not true!" Freddie sputtered.

"Oh, yeah? Then how come ever since Ông Ngoại got kidnapped, you haven't asked for my help once?

Or even my opinion? Every time I've tried to contribute, I'm told to sit back. I can help too, you know! You keep pushing me aside like everyone else. You have never even given me a chance. Well, guess what—I'm not a baby."

"You certainly are acting like one!" Freddie felt her own anger creep up. "Look what happens when you do things your way! You almost got mauled by a tiger!"

"That was *your* fault to begin with!" Liên refused to back down. "And if I didn't make a run for it, Duy never would have had a chance to scare it off with the motorcycle. You don't know everything, Freddie. Just because you went away to America doesn't mean you can come back here and act like nothing has changed. The fact is, things *have* changed. *I've* changed. And I'm not going to play the same clumsy brainiac role that you and everyone else wants me to. You haven't been here. You haven't been around. This is my home—and it hasn't been yours for a long time."

A stifling silence fell over the feuding cousins.

"Wow" was all Freddie could say. She felt a sting worse than a tiger's bite.

She knew Liên was upset, but she didn't think her cousin was capable of hurting her like that. Maybe Liên was right; maybe there *was* more to Liên than Freddie realized.

"Fine, then," Freddie conceded. "If you think you can find Ông Ngoại, go for it. I'm done making the decisions, because apparently everything I do isn't good enough. I'm not going with you."

From behind the mud-streaked lenses of Liên's glasses, Freddie could see Liên's eyes tearing up. Without saying a word, Liên spun on her heels and headed deeper into the jungle. Freddie watched Liên for as long as she could before she couldn't track her any longer. Freddie exhaled, finding her breath. She wasn't used to being the rational one. This new role was something she had to get used to. But she could admit to herself she was snapping at her cousin a lot. The hunger. The stress. The desperation. It was all getting to them. It was all getting to her.

But the regret was instant. Freddie wanted to apologize for everything, even if she still wasn't sure what even happened. She wanted to go back to sipping sugarcane drinks. She wanted to go back to goofing off on the beach and splitting bánh mì. But more than that, she didn't want one of the most important people in her world to hate her.

Freddie started after Liên, but Duy reached out and

grabbed Freddie's shoulder. "Let her cool off," he said. "Give her some space."

She shrugged off Duy's grasp. "I don't care if it's what she needs right now. I'll give her all the space she wants once we're out of this jungle. But there's a tiger on the loose and I don't just mean that muscley goon with a rifle."

Freddie took off in Liên's direction. It was morning now, but very early—still caught in a bit of night sky. The sun was only a sliver, mixing the sky with purples, oranges, and pinks. Liên had a bit of a headstart. How was Freddie going to find her.

It didn't take long for Freddie to get her answer.

She heard a scream—Liên's scream.

Freddie raced in the direction of the scream. It was back toward the waterfall with the turtle. She ignored the branches cutting across her cheek as she charged ahead. Her toe caught on a gnarled root which sent her flying to the ground. She didn't feel any pain. She just needed to reach Liên.

She stopped herself when just before she reached the clearing, ducking behind a group of rocks.

There was Liên. She was behind held in place by Con Hổ.

And next to him was Nhất.

CHAPTER 16

Freddie was stuck. She could try and make a run back to the cave to notify Duy. But that would mean leaving Liên alone, and that wasn't an option.

Nhất knelt by the stream, bringing a handful of water to his mouth. His jacket was folded neatly on a rock. The sleeves of his dress shirt were cuffed to his elbows. He took another drink of water before washing his face.

"Ah, that's refreshing," Nhất said, flicking the remnants of water from his hands. "I was worried when I didn't find you all the way out here. I thought something might have happened to you and your cousin. Thirst. Hunger. A run-in with a nasty krait. Or, heaven forbid, you uncovered an old, forgotten land mine."

Nhất walked up to Liên who was still thrashing in Con Hổ's grip. "I'd save your energy if I were you. Being left in a remote jungle without the strength to find your way out is a death sentence."

Liên stopped kicking. Her body relaxed.

"Now tell me, con. Where's the other one?"

Freddie gripped the edge of the rock, almost as if it was the only thing keeping her from barreling into Nhất and Con Hổ. She had to get Duy. Maybe he could talk to his father, make an exchange for Ông Ngoại and Liên. At this point, Freddie didn't care—Nhất could have the crossbow.

But she didn't have to make a decision. One was already being made for her.

Duy stepped out of the bushes and into the clearing. "Ba, why are you here? I told you I . . . I was handling them."

Freddie's heart dropped to her stomach. Liên had been right. Duy was on his father's side all along. She searched for some explanation in his eyes, but his gaze was locked onto his father, his expression just as cold. Duy wasn't giving Freddie anything.

Nhất scoffed. "You've been out here playing around." He gestured to Duy's bamboo sling. "And thriving, I see."

Duy lowered his head, his jaw muscles clenching. "Where's their grandfather?"

Nhất grinned. "He's back in Đà Nẵng, waiting. But I did promise him that I'd return his granddaughters in exchange for his information. Where's the other one?"

Freddie sucked in a breath.

Duy shook his head. "I lost her."

"Ngu con bò!" Nhất spat. He raised his hand, poised to strike.

Duy flinched. "But I can find her! I know where she went!"

"Good," said Nhất after a moment, lowering his hand. "We need her. She can't be spilling our secrets. Go—get out of my sight. The professor will just have to talk if he wants at least one of his granddaughters to live through this."

"No!" Liên flailed. "Let me go!"

Freddie could only watch. They were going to take Liên from her, and there was nothing she could do. Her throat throbbed, but she refused to cry.

"Once you find her, bring her back to Đà Nẵng," Nhất instructed. "Even you can handle something as simple as that, can't you?"

Duy nodded, his eyes trained on the ground.

Nhất signaled for Con Hổ to follow as he made his way back to the caravan. The last thing Freddie saw before Con Hổ dragged Liên away was the look in her eyes. That look of terror would be burned in her brain forever.

And with that, Freddie felt alone. Alone in the jungle. A sickening fear found its way to her throat. Her breathing got shorter, faster.

With Nhất gone, Duy turned to look at Freddie. She started to run, but Duy was faster. He wrapped his arms around her.

Freddie tried to wrestle her way out of Duy's grip. "Get off me!"

"Wait!" He whispered, putting a finger to his lips and gripping her tighter.

They waited until they couldn't hear anything. Finally Freddie shoved Duy and stepped away as far as she could until her back touched a tree trunk. "So Liên was right about you all along. You really *are* with them!"

Finally, Duy braved a look at Freddie. The icy stare had melted away and in its place was a soft sadness. "Come on, Freddie. Use your head. If I did anything to disobey my father back there, we'd all be done for. Con Hổ was going to find us eventually . . . that's his job, and he's very, very good at it. But I promise you I didn't signal them where we were. I really am trying to help. It was all an act."

"You're telling me." Deep down though, Freddie knew Duy was making sense. He could have handed her over to Nhất right then and there, but he hadn't.

"You have to trust me," he said. "It's not over yet. We still have a chance." Duy held up the diary.

"Who cares about that?"

Duy shook his head, placing his palm on the diary. "Your ông ngoại insisted that all the answers are in here. You trust him, right? Then trust me too."

Freddie sighed, slumping. "Not like I have a choice, right?"

"I mean . . . I'd like you to trust me because we're friends." Duy stood over her. She'd forgotten how much bigger he was than she. Imposing, but not intentionally. He stuck out his hand.

She reached out and took it, allowing him to pull her to her feet. "If I'm going to trust you, I'm going to need you to trust me," said Freddie, thinking back on her encounter in the oasis. "When I ran out to find you water, I saw something here. It was like . . . a vision." She took a breath. "The golden turtle."

She waited for Duy to laugh, but he stared back at her, waiting for her to continue. He acted like it was the most normal thing anyone could say. "Go on."

"It appeared in front of this waterfall. And it said that we're on the right path, but that we need to return the crossbow," Freddie continued. "But . . ."

"But what?"

"But it has to be returned by the king."

"The king is dead."

"I *know*," Freddie said, annoyed. "The turtle said that 'his blood lives on.' Don't get me started on this guy and his riddles. He also said that I have 'the gift,' but I have no idea what he's talking about."

Duy exhaled, puffing his cheeks. "I may know *some*thing."

Freddie looked at him curiously.

"You saw me have one of my nightmares last night."

"Yeah. It was scary." She wasn't sure what Duy's nightmares had to do with the turtle's command.

"I've had them all my life," Duy explained. "Not only me, but my dad, and even my ông nội." He turned away and sighed. "I'm going to tell you something, and you have to promise not to freak out."

"I promise nothing."

Duy rolled his eyes. "The nightmares I have are really all the same nightmare over and over again. I'm standing on a fortress, looking out over a battlefield."

"Go on," Freddie said, imitating Duy.

"At first, I see glistening spear tips and lances, then I hear the beating of the war drums. They're so loud, but not louder than the screams. Screams from all of these soldiers. Then flashes of golden light pouring down all around, but the screams never stop."

Freddie couldn't help but shiver at the picture Duy was painting. "That's exactly what I saw in the turtle's vision!"

"It's the crossbow," Duy continued. "These nightmares are tied to the crossbow, I'm sure of it. The obsession is like a family tradition. Or a curse. My family is . . . messed up. And it has been ever since my ancestor first held the crossbow in his hands."

"Wait. Waitwaitwaitwaitwait," said Freddie, pinching the bridge of her nose. "Are you telling me that you're like . . . some *descendant* of King An Dương?"

Duy didn't say a word, but his eyes conveyed everything Freddie needed to know.

Freddie shook her head. "This whole thing keeps

getting weirder and weirder. But I guess I shouldn't be surprised by anything at this point."

Duy continued. "These nightmares, or the curse, or whatever it is . . . it's been passed down through my family's bloodline. A little at a time, bit by bit, it chokes you—transforms you into something unrecognizable. It transformed my ông nội. It happened to my dad. And it's happening to me."

"You think the crossbow has some kind of magical hold over your dad too?"

"I do." Duy looked away. "You've seen how my dad is. My grandfather was the same way, and I've heard that his dad was too. And I feel it starting to take over me."

"How are you so sure?" Freddie asked.

"Because no one would willingly do"—still, Duy refused to look at her—"the things my dad does."

In that moment, Freddie wanted to throw her arms around Duy and wrap him in a big hug. She could tell from the twitch of his frown that he was suffering. And there was nothing she could do about it. "What are you saying?" asked Freddie. "You really think you and your family . . . you're cursed?"

"Yeah, I guess I am."

"Maybe we both are." Freddie slumped against the

wall. "This whole thing is all my fault. Liên was right. I come back here after being away all this time and this happens."

"That's not fair."

"Yeah, well, look where it got us. Liên ran off and got captured, and now she's gone, and it's all because of me." Freddie felt a hot tear roll down her cheek. She tried to measure her quavering voice. She sniffed, hoping that would dam the tears, but they kept coming. "I dunno. I guess I wanted to prove that I could be useful, you know? Like, I'm back here, home again, and it feels like home, and yet it doesn't, and I thought I knew who I was, but I'm here with my family and I act like a complete doofus. I can't even understand or speak with them. I'm like this weird ghost floating in the background, on the outside." Freddie chewed the tip of her thumbnail. "I should have trusted her. I should have done more."

"You did everything you could. There's nothing more you could have done," said Duy. "Con Hổ would have found her. He did—he found us. But I don't want you to worry—my dad is . . ." Duy paused, carefully thinking over his next words. "My dad is not a good person, but he's not going to hurt her. He's only after the crossbow. Liên and your ông ngoại will be fine."

Freddie sighed. It wasn't much, but it was a crumb of comfort she could hold onto. For now.

"Well, now what, Your Highness?" Freddie asked with a bow.

"Ha. Ha," said Duy, his scowl back in full force.

"Seriously. What do we do?"

Duy shrugged. "We go to Đà Nẵng."

CHAPTER 17

Freddie and Duy wasted no time packing. They doused the fire and stuffed Duy's backpack with the few items they had left. Duy was in no shape to drive, given that his arm was still stuck in a makeshift bamboo sling, so it was up to Freddie. She pushed the bike out of the cave and headed north using Duy's compass until they found the road. It had taken Freddie a minute to get used to driving the motorbike—first, they had to navigate their way through a jungle, but she surprised herself by getting the hang of it fairly quickly, like riding a, well, regular bike, but with a motor. And why shouldn't she? Plenty of other Vietnamese teenagers were driving motorbikes like it was in their DNA.

Đà Nẵng wasn't far by motorcycle—only a few hours. Freddie had to remind herself to keep focused on the road as her mind kept daydreaming about all the food she'd eat, or the feeling of burying herself in a fluffy bed topped with fresh sheets, or indulging in a very, very long, warm shower. Neither she nor Duy had any idea what they'd do when they reached the city; they had to get there first. Freddie couldn't help but laugh. This kind of improvisation would've driven Liên crazy.

"You know, I kind of, sort of remember visiting Đà Nẵng once," said Freddie, her hair whipping in the wind.

"Well, despite our circumstances, you're in for a treat," said Duy. "I'm jealous you get to experience it for the first time all over again. It's changed quite a bit since you were last here. The whole country has. A lot more buildings. A lot more construction."

It was late in the afternoon by the time Freddie and Duy puttered into Đà Nẵng. The city's iconic Rồng Bridge was a welcoming sight. The yellow dragon sculpture arched and curved to form a heavily trafficked bridge crossing the Hàn River. It was still light out, but according to Duy, in a few hours, the enormous dragon head would spew a ball of fire while tourists and locals alike snapped pictures.

In the harbor, double decker tour ships packed with partygoers glided by humble fishing boats—a blend of new and old. Then the rest of the city came into full view. Freddie had no idea seeing that much concrete would bring her so much joy.

Đà Nẵng was a completely different vibe from the sleepy seaside town of Vỏ Rùa Làng. Despite it being a beach destination, there was an undeniable frenetic, urban energy. Towering skyscrapers lined the shores with plenty of blinking LED signs vying to grab peoples' attention. Vietnam was magical in that sense: You could transport yourself to a remote, sprawling jungle and only a few hours later find yourself in a bustling, concrete metropolis. An endless, intimidating, exciting, buzzing sea of motorcyclists whizzed by her as she struggled to keep up with the crushing tide.

"You're doing great," Duy said, sensing her hesitation. "Keep your head on a swivel, your speed steady. Blend in with the flow and you'll be alright."

His words of encouragement seemed to do the trick. Freddie maneuvered the bike into the stream of traffic, following the crowd like she was part of a school of fish.

Freddie's attention was drawn to an enormous Ferris

wheel and a nearby roofless building adorned with soft glowing red and yellow lanterns. A street-food fair. Booths were lined up with puffs of meaty-smelling smoke billowing from their sizzling grills.

"That looks promising . . ." Freddie flashed a cheesy smile over her shoulder.

"Okay." Duy nodded in surrender. "Let's stop here."

A short time later, Freddie and Duy stood before the tents, struggling to choose which meal they wanted to be their first since returning to civilization. Duy counted the đồng in his pocket, his brow furrowing with concern.

"Not a whole lot of money to work with here," he informed. "Enough for food, but not enough for a place to crash . . ."

Freddie swiped the đồng from Duy's hands. "That's a later problem. Food now!"

They carefully checked out the selection of every booth. Freddie passed on the steamed balut topped with cilantro and crushed peanuts, even after Duy called her a coward. They finally decided to get a variety of small dishes to split. Freddie carried her plastic tray past a stage where a band was setting up to do a live set. As they made their way to a free table, a rowdy group of kids with shaved heads and crew cuts wearing oversized jerseys and kicking around a ragged soccer ball nearly ran her over, but Freddie was too hungry to care. Her mouth watered as she took a moment to admire their bounty: a bowl of mì quảng; a steaming pile of grilled morning glory; and, for dessert, a bowl of chè with creamy coconut milk sloshing over the sides.

But after crushing up a speckled toasted sesame rice cracker over the dark yellow noodles, Freddie couldn't eat despite her hunger. She only stared down at her bowl.

"What's wrong?" asked Duy. "Why aren't you eating?"

"Liên and Ông Ngoại are out there. Somewhere. How can I slurp noodles knowing they're still being held captive somewhere in the city?"

"Well, you aren't going to do them any good if you don't have any energy. You have to eat. Choke it down if you have to."

Freddie plucked a pair of black chopsticks from the metal tin in the center of the table. He was right. She needed to eat something. "It would make all this easier if I knew my cousin didn't hate my guts."

"She doesn't hate you," said Duy. "Now *me* on the other hand . . ."

"You saw how she looked at me when she got taken from the cave."

"Look, I'm the last person you should be going to for this kind of advice." Duy set his chopsticks down and wiped his mouth with a napkin. "I'm not exactly a people-person, but, you know, sometimes the easiest solution is right in front of you. What does Liên need? And can you give it to her? Figure that out and give it to her."

Freddie stirred her noodles, thinking. She'd have to let that marinate for a bit. "Yeah, I see what you mean. I think. Thanks."

"No problem."

"What about your dad?" Freddie asked, changing the subject. "I don't know about you, but I haven't seen any sight of your dad's fancy SUV or a caravan of any type today. How are we going to find where they went? What *are* we going to do?"

"There's not much we can do tonight," Duy admitted. "I say we find a place to sleep and start fresh in the morning."

Freddie slurped down the last bites of noodles then tossed back a quail egg. "I still have a little left in me to keep looking."

"Let's get to it then."

They spent another two hours driving around Đà Nẵng looking for any sign of Nhất, Con Hổ, or Nhất's caravan of minions, but nothing looked promising. At least Freddie's fear of crashing the bike into traffic had gone away; she was practically an expert driver now. Freddie wondered if her mom would let her apply for a motorcycle license someday.

Freddie allowed herself to get lost—after all, she wasn't even sure what she was supposed to be looking for. It seemed as though the city's blocks were structured like one giant department store: one block housed stores selling gardening supplies while another block sold motorbikes and bike paraphernalia and another block was where you could find used books spilling from carts with bowed axles straining under their weight. All these stores were family-owned. Freddie hardly saw any chain stores. Unlike back home, here she could count the number of McDonald's and Jollibees she passed on one hand.

There was a frenetic energy to the city as the evening stretched on. The streets came alive with Đà Nẵng's youth flooding the sidewalks, ordering skewered meats from stand-alone carts, and sipping fruit drinks. Teenage boys dressed in polo shirts and sandals drove their mopeds while their girlfriends, wearing their best weekend dresses, casually rode sidesaddle on the back with their legs crossed, checking their makeup. Everyone was smiling, enjoying the warm seaside breeze on a perfect summer night. Freddie twisted and turned down alleys, rumbling past more food carts where customers indulged in a late-night meal straight from Styrofoam take-out boxes and drivers catching a quick snooze while balanced on their bikes. She paused briefly to take in the calming, monotone chants floating out an ornate temple's open windows.

Finally, Duy tapped Freddie's shoulder, directing her to pull over at the front of a church. It was a giant cathedral that looked like a birthday cake; it was the color of pink frosting and topped with a rooster weathervane. Freddie and Duy found a bench around the back underneath a tree blooming with clumps of purple blossoms. They sat slumped against each other in front of a grotto. A marble table covered with rows of lit candles provided a comforting glow.

"I'm beat," said Freddie. "I can't keep my eyes open."

"We can rest here a bit," said Duy, trying his best to fight back a yawn.

Freddie watched the candles flicker in the gentle summer breeze. "What is this place?"

"A Catholic church," Duy explained. "They call it the Con Gà Church. Because of the—"

"Rooster on top," said Freddie. Apparently her Vietnamese *was* coming back to her. "Con gà. I get it."

"Well, it's more of an iconic Đà Nẵng tourist attraction. Kind of like the Dragon Bridge, or Non Nước, or that bridge where all the couples cover the pier with heart-shaped locks." Duy nodded to a group of teens taking group selfies. "Lots of people come in and out here . . ."

Freddie lit up, catching on. "Oh! When you meant to *rest* here, you meant we're *sleeping* here."

"We'll be fine. No one pays attention to who leaves and who stays," winked Duy. He knelt next to a small, easy-to-miss window—and, thankfully, it was unlocked. After a quick look to make sure the coast was clear, Freddie and Duy slipped inside. They found themselves in the church's basement. There wasn't much to it. Freddie spotted stacks of metal folding chairs, a row of rusty lockers, and some discarded music stands. But most importantly, Freddie found a small bathroom with a stand-in shower stall. She took her time, letting the hot water rinse off all the dirt she had accumulated over the past two days. Freddie made a promise never to take running water for granted ever again.

Freddie finally got out of the shower, stepping aside so Duy could take his turn. He had already set up two sleeping areas—two blankets laid out on the floor along with two pillows. Her pillow was flat, but she wasn't about to complain. Anything was better than sleeping on a cave floor. She tossed her borrowed áo dài along with Duy's clothes into a rattly washer and dryer. A donation bin had provided Freddie a clean pair of baggy shorts and large T-shirt—the perfect impromptu pajamas.

It was another muggy evening. A bead of sweat dripped down her arms. She could still hear the sounds of people outside, a few stragglers roaming the court-yard. Somewhere not too far away, a vendor was hawking his wares using a scratchy megaphone. She'd thought that the sporadic beeping of motorbike horns would be annoying, but she actually found them comforting. The lulling sounds of night in the city.

Duy settled in, resetting his chin in his hand while he flipped through the diary. He did so with the greatest care, making sure to turn them using his pointer and thumb, as if he were afraid the pages would crumble at his touch. His brows furrowed and he scratched the back of his head, deep in concentration.

Freddie sat cross-legged across from him. "I don't know how you're reading that. If we didn't have to get up early tomorrow to find this legendary crossbow, I'd plan on sleeping for a million years."

"Can't sleep."

"Right. The nightmares." Freddie cracked open a tin of ointment that she found in the bathroom's medicine cabinet and rubbed some of it on her bruised ribs. The distinct spicy medicinal scent filled the basement air. Then she waved the can at Duy. "You want some of this?"

"Tiger Balm!" Duy blushed and turned back to the book. "No, I'm fine."

Freddie rolled her eyes and tossed it to him, which he caught with his good arm. "Don't be stubborn about this."

Duy swirled some of the ointment underneath his sleeve. "Ooh, yeah, there's that tingle." He looked tired. He'd given up on trying to contain his ponytail, so his hair was wild and splayed down around his shoulders.

"Well, give it to me straight," said Freddie. "You said all the answers would be in here. Did my ông ngoại leave us any crumbs to follow?"

"It's . . . complicated."

"Shocker."

"What I mean is, based on his notes, your ông ngoại is fairly confident that the crossbow was left on a beach. The most consistent records indicate that this all went down in Nghệ An province at one of Diễn Châu's beaches. And according to the journal, your grandfather spent years searching for the crossbow in that area. Then he expanded his search, moving south—*a lot* farther south."

Freddie nodded intently. She was with him so far.

"Finally, we know that your grandfather told my dad to head to Đà Nẵng. The problem is, your grandfather writes that he's searched every major beach in Đà Nẵng more than once. So if he didn't find Nỏ Định Mệnh during all those times, why is he so convinced it's here?"

"Your guess is as good as mine," said Freddie. "So what do we do?"

Duy threw a frustrated hand through his hair. "Everything goes back to the original legend, so I figure we start there. We know that the tale ends on the shores of an ocean. That's where Cao Lỗ found the bodies of King An Dương, Princess Mị Châu, Prince Trọng

Thủy . . . and the crossbow. I guess we *could* retrace your ông ngoại's steps and take another look at all the beaches in Đà Nẵng, but we don't have that kind of time."

Freddie took the diary, allowing a flurry of paper to flutter out. It was a mess of various lists, scraps, and maps. It seemed as though Ông Ngoại had jotted down and kept every thought that had come to him.

She plucked a list from the pile. Each bullet point named a beach. "How many beaches are in Đà Nẵng, anyway?"

"Who knows? Tons. The whole city is practically a beach. But that's not counting all the little, hidden, secret beaches that I'm sure aren't even on anyone's radar. It would take us forever to find them all."

Freddie dragged her finger down the list of beaches. Something stuck out to her. "Wait a second. Non Nước? You said that was a tourist attraction. Nước means water—as in . . . a beach? Ông Ngoại crossed it off here"—she flipped a few more pages in the diary—"but then he writes it again here, then he scratches it out, and then here again with a question mark."

"It's a beach, sure, but it's also Ngũ Hành Sơn—you know, the Marble Mountains?" said Duy. "Sorry, I guess that's a little confusing. All the locals refer to them as the Non Nước Mountains."

Freddie laughed. That was the Vietnamese language for you—it had its own ebb and flow. The words changed. The meanings shifted.

Where had she heard that before? Freddie's fingers dropped down to her wrist where she felt the cool touch of her grandfather's bracelet. Ông Ngoại had talked about change when he recounted the legend of the crossbow to Freddie and Liên the night before the ceremony. His words echoed in Freddie's mind:

The thing about these old stories is that they shift after being passed down from generation to generation. They evolve. You could say that these legends are a reflection of our own lives. You must adapt. You must pivot.

Maybe Freddie needed to change her perspective—to think about this puzzle in a different way.

That's when it hit her. Freddie shot up, a tingling sensation frizzled through her.

"What? What is it?" asked Duy.

She began pacing, chewing her thumb. Her stomach flip-flopped with excitement. Her heart raced. The hairs on her arms tingled. "Follow me on this. What if everyone has been thinking about the legend too literally? We know that the legend ended at a place with water—with nước. But what if the final battle with the crossbow didn't take place on the typical beaches that we normally think of—the ones people vacation at with big beach umbrellas, facing the ocean, things like that."

Duy scratched the back of his neck. "I don't get it."

"Technically, literally speaking . . . a beach is just a piece of land at the edge of water, right? What if the final battle took place on a different kind of beach? There are many different types of beaches. Is there a beach at the Non Nước Mountains? Could it be . . . I dunno . . . hidden? Buried? What if the beach that the legend talks about is—"

"*Under* the Marble Mountains . . ." Duy slapped his forehead. "Whoa. I never thought about that before but . . . it's certainly possible. I gotta sit down."

"You are sitting down."

"Then I gotta stand up." Duy sprung to his feet and joined Freddie pacing. "It's the best lead we've got. I say we go for it. They aren't too far from us. We go straight there first thing tomorrow morning."

"Sounds like a plan." Freddie settled back down on

the makeshift bed and lay back on her pancake pillow, putting her hands behind her head.

"Hey, Freddie," said Duy. "I was thinking about what that turtle said . . . about you having *the gift*. Maybe it was referring to your puzzle solving ability."

Freddie blushed. "Ha. You think?"

"Maybe." Duy shrugged. "But even if that's not the case, you don't have to prove yourself to anybody—not even your family. You're pretty amazing just how you are."

Freddie turned away, hiding her smile.

CHAPTER 18

The smell of fresh coffee woke Freddie up. She blinked awake and the first thing she saw was Duy's grinning face.

"Ahh!" she shouted, surprised.

"Sorry," said Duy. "Didn't mean to scare you."

"Personal space, bud." She grabbed a tall glass filled with the familiar thick layer of sweetened condensed milk stuck to the bottom and the dark brown coffee floating on top. Cà phê sữa đá. Life blood. Her mom never let her have it, but Freddie was a hero among her friends whenever she'd sneak an order for everyone after school.

Duy watched in both disgust and fascination as she

guzzled it down. "You know you're supposed to stir that first right?"

"Need coffee. Don't care."

Duy was already packed and ready to head for the Marble Mountains, not that there was much to pack. It didn't take long for Freddie to change into her freshly washed and dried áo dài. Before Freddie stepped out the door, she took another look in the mirror. Her durian bruise was fading and the cuts on her face had almost completely vanished. Freddie turned her chin, angling this way and that. Even though she was healing, she didn't look the same as before. Something had changed. She looked . . . older somehow.

Freddie expected the trip to the mountains would take them most of the morning, but it turned out that the Marble Mountains were practically inside the city. They were actually made up of five different marble and limestone hills that housed beautiful Buddhist sanctuaries. Lots of tourists clamored there to check out the hidden nooks and to soak in the spectacular views of the city. She knew it was a popular destination, but she didn't anticipate the Marble Mountains being *that* popular.

"This really *is* a tourist hot spot." Freddie gawked as minivans packed with families inched their way to the crowded parking lot. A group of children in short-sleeved button ups and shorts ran past, followed by a very tired-looking camp counselor holding a flag.

Freddie and Duy strolled past giant buses as they unloaded floods of tourists. The air filled with people talking in all different languages: German, Italian, Japanese, and probably even more that she didn't recognize. It seemed like everyone was posing and taking pictures in front of the entrance. They passed stands selling miniature animal carvings supposedly made from the rock in the mountains and vending machines stocked with ice cream and cold drinks. A lady used an old butcher knife to lop off the tops of coconuts for drinks. Mothers fed their squirmy children from boxed lunches while treating themselves to double swirl ice creams. It seemed so strange that all these people were going about their day, some coming from different countries on vacation, completely oblivious of the very serious danger that was brewing right under their feet.

"Maybe I was wrong," said Freddie, watching a mother pushing a baby stroller past them. "There's no way it could be here, right? I mean, it's a tourist spot. How many people do you think visit here and no one has stumbled upon the crossbow? They have no idea they could be walking right above a magical ancient relic."

"Hiding in plain sight. It's brilliant. No one would think to—" Suddenly Duy stopped, realization spreading across his face. "We've got company."

Freddie turned in the direction Duy had been looking. Two guards stood far beyond a barrier that restricted guests to the designated path. A man and a woman, both dressed in the same uniform as the man who had sold Freddie and Duy their tickets—crisp, light blue button-up shirts tucked into navy slacks with brown dress shoes—stood next to an area roped off by caution tape.

"Who? Them?" Freddie asked.

"Don't look straight at them!" Duy warned, turning his face into his shoulder. "Don't let them see you. I recognize them. Those people don't work for the park—they work for my dad. He's here, and I bet he's got the entire mountain crawling with his people."

"But they're just . . . standing there."

"No, they're guarding something. See—I said not to look directly at them!" he stressed again. "Okay, there . . . you see? They're next to a hole. I bet you anything that's where we need to go. Down."

A shiver ran up Freddie's spine. She was eager to get moving. Her stomach was twisted in knots at the enormous task they were about to undertake. Liên and Ông Ngoại were somewhere in there waiting for her.

As they moved deeper into the mountain, Freddie understood why it was such a popular destination. Wide-open, enormous echoing chambers housed beautiful, intricate stone statues and shrines. You never knew what to expect when you took a new path leading to a new tunnel to explore. The steep, narrow stone steps fluctu-ated in width, causing Freddie to feel a bit light-headed. Despite Freddie being unable to read the plaques, she understood there was some serious history here.

"You know, during the war, they built hospitals in these mountains," said Duy. "The American army never knew about them."

"Guess these mountains are used to keeping secrets," said Freddie.

It wasn't long before Freddie felt a few drops of water hit her head. Soon the dirt was covered in dark spots. The sunny afternoon was about to get a lot less sunny.

Freddie waited for a young mother and child to pass as they admired the dripping stalactites. "What's the plan?"

"We wait a little longer. The last thing we want to happen is to get caught before we even get inside."

When the last group of tourists dashed to the exit using their maps and brochures as umbrellas, Freddie knew it was time to enact their plan. Duy checked his watch. "The park is closing. Now's our chance."

An instrumental version of "The Sound of Silence" crackled over speakers hidden in the shrubs. Duy led Freddie back to the area where they spotted Nhất's guards, but this time there wasn't any sight of them— only a dead-end designated by a bamboo rail. On the other side of the partition was a large hole that led down deeper into a pitch-black chamber. A coil of thick rope that had been dropped down into the hole was securely wrapped around a tree.

Duy gripped the rope, testing it. "Looks like they used ten millimeter climbing rope. Our lucky day. This should hold." He looked up at Freddie with a shrug. "I'm pretty sure, anyway."

Freddie gave the rope a sharp tug. Nice and secure. She hoped. Her hands started to sweat. Was she really going to do this?

"We'll need to make a harness out of the rope," Duy said, then walked her through the process. Freddie threaded the rope through her legs and wrapped it around her waist. "If you remember to lean back all the way down, there shouldn't be any issue. You go first, then I'll go."

Freddie took one hesitant look down. "Wish me luck," she said, closing her eyes.

"You'll be fine," Duy reassured her.

But Freddie wasn't so sure.

CHAPTER 19

The deep descent seemed to go on forever. Freddie felt a chill each time she went a little further down. The cool cave air was a welcome escape from the muggy, summer heat. Any time she started to feel a creeping panic bud in her chest, she refocused her gaze on Duy. From above, he gave her a resassuring thumbs up. If he was nervous, he didn't show any signs of it. And she wasn't about to show fear in front of him.

Eventually, her feet touched the ground. She stepped out of the makeshift harness allowing Duy to pull the rope back up so that he could repel down. He managed the task well enough, muffling his grunts and winces as best he could. Not bad for someone with only one functioning arm.

Now that they were at the bottom level, there was only one way to go. In the distance, Freddie heard a rumbling throughout the cavern. Rocks being crushed. Jackhammers, maybe? Duy put his finger to his lips and continued down the tunnel. She placed her hand on the wall and followed it.

The tunnel opened up to a massive, multi-tiered chamber. Massive stalactites dripped from the cave ceiling, stretching out like bony claws. It was like walking into an empty museum. Moonlight spilled through the hole in the ceiling, covering the cave in a ghastly glow. When the raindrops fell through the beam of the light, the drops twinkled like tiny diamonds. High up above, a smattering of stars peeked out from behind the dark clouds. Even though they were deep underground, there were still the sporadic sounds of animals chirping, cooing, and cawing.

Nhất had certainly wasted no time getting his workers to tear up the cavern searching for the crossbow. Construction flood lights powered by rumbling generators were stationed every few yards so that the whole area lit up like a football stadium. How Nhất was able to transfer all the equipment this far into the depths of the mountain, Freddie didn't have a clue, but she assumed money was the answer. Duy wasn't kidding—his family had money and lots of it to burn.

"Any sight of Liên or Ông Ngoại?" asked Freddie. "I don't see them."

Nhất's hired hands scurried about like ants. There were a lot of them. She estimated at least fifty. Probably more.

Duy squinted in an attempt to get a better look. Then he sprang up, tapping Freddie's shoulders and pointing. "Look! Right over there. See that table?"

Freddie's heart pounded in her throat. She could only nod. Nhất had set up a wooden table and some chairs. Ông Ngoại sat in one chair, his hands clasped in front of him, bound with twine. He was still wearing his suit from the ceremony, but it was ruffled, ripped in places and with bits of cotton poking out. His wild hair looked more disheveled than it usually did. Con Hổ stood guard, his default impatient frown planted on his face as he flipped a massive serrated, black-bladed hunting knife in the air. Liên was positioned in front of Con Hổ. She had no injuries, at least from what Freddie could see, although one of her round glasses lenses had a crack down the middle. Overall, Ông Ngoại and Liên seemed to be okay, at least physically, and that was good enough for the moment.

Ông Ngoại and Liên were so close! It took everything in Freddie not to bolt out and go for it. But Liên's voice echoed in her head: rushing in without a plan didn't seem like the right move anymore.

She took a breath and steadied herself. "What about the crossbow? Are we too late?"

"I've got nothing," Duy said.

Freddie watched helplessly as Nhất paced behind Ông Ngoại.

"Where is it, old man?" asked Nhất. "My patience wears thin."

"I've told you everything I know. I led you here, didn't I?" said Ông Ngoại. "All I know is that it's down here somewhere. That's my best guess. It has to be."

"For your sake, I hope so. You and your granddaughter are not leaving this cave until it is found," growled Nhất. "And if you're sealed up along with 'your best guess' . . . so be it."

"Duy, we have to hurry," said Freddie, pushing down her panic. She didn't want to know what would happen when Nhất's patience ran out.

"Good news: they don't know where the crossbow is." Duy's eyes darted about the cavern. "Bad news is neither do we. Any ideas?"

"I think we're looking for anything that could be a beach." Freddie scanned the area. That was when she saw exactly what she was looking for. Not too far from where they were perched was an unassuming pool of water. A beach! Technically. An underground beach. And no one was guarding it. "That's gotta be it, right?"

"Only one way to find out," said Duy.

Freddie helped guide Duy down the slope and then followed him as they crouch-walked, using a bulldozer as cover. Nhất must have his excavation team searching another area of the cavern. At the edge of the shore, Freddie peered into the pool and saw there was a tunnel opening at the far end of the water. If they were going to take this chance, they had to go—now.

They looked over their shoulders to make sure they weren't being watched and then waded into the pool; the further they walked, the deeper it got. The water quickly reached Freddie's chin and she had to dog-paddle a bit as the sandy ground gave way. Duy was able to tiptoe, trying his best to keep his bamboo sling from getting completely submerged, but they were just barely able to keep their noses above the water under the tunnel's low ceiling.

Before Freddie knew it, the tunnel opened up once again and they resurfaced in another chamber. A hidden pocket. Light somehow managed to pour in from a hole in the ceiling, bathing the unassuming underground beach in an otherworldly glow.

Freddie gasped. Her hand went to her mouth as she spotted the skeletons half buried in the sand. She had found it. The final resting place of the king, the princess, and the prince. This was where King An Dương and Princess Mị Châu had tried to escape the pursuing army. This is where Prince Trọng Thủy and King An Dương dueled to the end. And this is where Cao Lỗ found the newborn prince and the crossbow. A sense of wonder, awe, and a bit of melancholy rippled through the air. The scene before them almost looked as if it was carefully staged like the final act of a Greek tragedy. A beautiful, painful moment frozen in time.

Somehow, the royal clothes they wore were still in tact. Maybe the cool depths of the cave provided the perfect climate to preserve the ancient robes. The king's skeleton still gripped his sword, now covered with barnacles. Freddie couldn't help but feel a twinge of pity for him—even after all this time, he couldn't let go of his tragic past.

Freddie watched as Duy stood before the remains. She walked up and placed a hand on his shoulder. "You okay?"

"Yeah," he nodded. "It's pretty weird seeing my grandfather. My great, great, great, great, great—"

"I get it," said Freddie, crouching next to the skeleton. "I don't see any sign of the crossbow, though." She jutted a thumb at the king's skull. "And he's not saying anything."

"Wait, Freddie!" said Duy. "Don't move. Look!"

Freddie's wrist was positioned right under the beam of light coming from the cave's ceiling. It seemed to reflect off the bracelet, creaking a stronger, more concentrated beam of light into a bit of sand directly in the middle of where the three skeletons lay—almost as if they formed a triangle around it.

Duy dropped to his knees and began digging. Freddie kept her bracelet under the light while trying to get a good look over Duy's shoulders. It didn't take long before Duy pulled something out of the hole.

It was an ornate wooden box. He brushed the sand away, using his fingers to get the remnants out of the grooves. He looked at Freddie, as if waiting for permission. She nodded in return. Duy flipped the brass clap, opened the lid, and—

There it was.

Nỏ Định Mệnh. The Crossbow of Destiny.

At first glance, it didn't look all that impressive—no twinkling magic aura or heavenly glow. But she could make out some intricate carvings and bits of dark green jade inlay. It was beautiful and ancient-looking for sure. But nothing about it screamed magic to her.

"I kinda thought we'd hear the sound of harps or angels singing or something," said Freddie, breaking the tension.

"I know, right?" Duy exhaled slowly. "I'm holding like a real piece of Vietnamese history here."

"Now what?" said Freddie.

"Let's get your grandpa and cousin back," said Duy, stuffing the crossbow in his backpack. "Back into the water."

They retracted their steps.

When Freddie emerged, she stared into the barrel of a pistol.

A pistol held by Nhất.

"Nice to see you again, con."

CHAPTER 20

Con Hổ pulled Freddie and Duy out from the water. Nhất kept his pistol trained on Freddie.

"Freddie!" Liên shouted.

Ông Ngoại gasped. "Don't hurt her!"

"I need to thank Con Hổ," Nhất began, ignoring them. "It was his idea to keep an extra set of eyes on you after we last departed. My son is not accomplished at a great many things, and I think it's safe to add lying to that ever-growing list." Nhất patted his manicured hand on the back of Duy's head. "So, you're the mysterious masked rider. Poetic, I suppose. It seems the *new* legend of the crossbow also hinges on betrayal."

Duy bowed his head in shame.

Nhất pocketed the pistol, then snatched the crossbow from the backpack. "Cảm ơn, con. You saved us a lot of time."

"Now that you have the crossbow," Freddie said. "Let my family go."

Nhất wasn't paying attention to what Freddie was saying. He ran his hand over the crossbow, his fingers gliding along the grooved carvings. His eyes flashed a twinge of gold. "I did it. Nỏ Định Mệnh is mine. Back in the hands of its rightful owner after all this time. Now . . . let's see if the legends are true."

Nhất raised the bow and aimed it at Freddie.

"No!" cried Ông Ngoại, struggling in his chair, as Liên shouted, "You can't!"

But there was no mercy. No final words.

Freddie braced herself.

Duy tried to throw himself in front of Freddie, but he wasn't quick enough.

Ông Ngoại and Liên's screams cut through the air.

Nhất pulled the trigger and—

Nothing.

Freddie braved opening one eye. Then the other.

Nhất frowned and held up the crossbow, inspecting it from all angles. There was no arrow. No golden light.

He cursed in Vietnamese, then he pushed his way through a wall of guards as Con Hổ followed behind. His face was beet red, twisted in anger,and spittle flew through the air as he screeched orders. "No mất rồi. Không phải ở đây!"

"Are you okay?" asked Duy.

"Shh, shh! I'm fine!" Freddie waved Duy off, struggling to hear the words and piece them together. "'No mất rồi. Không phải ở đây.'" She repeated the words, quickly making the translation. She brightened. "There's something wrong! Something is gone! Something is missing!"

Duy nodded. "But what?"

Nhất tossed the crossbow on the table, landing in front of Ông Ngoại. "What's wrong with it? Why isn't it working?"

Ông Ngoại said nothing. Freddie thought he might be stalling, or maybe this was a negotiation tactic to set them free.

"*Now*, old man!" Nhất said, lifting his hand in the air—a signal to his hired hands. They all raised their weapons. A warning. A threat.

Calmly, Ông Ngoại adjusted his glasses and took one look at the crossbow. Freddie thought she saw the faintest hint of a smirk. "It's missing the tumbler."

Nhất backhanded a glass bottle, sending it flying into some rocks, flinging bits of glass and water in all directions. "Spread out. The tumbler must be here somewhere. Start looking!"

On command, the guards ran in all different directions. Even the men standing behind Freddie and Duy left their post. The whine of drills and jackhammers whirred. Bulldozers grumbled alive. Nhất and Con Hổ returned to the table and continued their interrogation, all but forgetting about Freddie and Duy.

Freddie seized the moment, turning back to Duy. "Tumbler?"

Duy leaned in, keeping his voice low. "The turtle claw acted as the crossbow's tumbler, remember? That's where the power came from."

"What the heck is a tumbler?"

"How can you not know what a crossbow tumbler is?" Duy massaged his temples. "Your grandfather practically lived and breathed the crossbow. I refuse to believe that you never—"

"Just tell me!"

"It's like . . . both a lock and a key. Sort of." The look on Duy's face told Freddie he was searching for the best way to describe it. "A tumbler clamps down on the crossbow's string, pulling it taught, and locks it into place. So when you pull the trigger, the tumbler lifts to release the string and fires the arrow."

Freddie pictured the mechanism in her head. Another faint spark of an idea sputtered. It wasn't a great idea. It wasn't even a good idea. It was half of a sort of an idea.

"Duy, what were the *exact* words Cao Lỗ said when he arrived at the beach?"

"What's with the pop quiz all of a sudden?"

"Come on, Duy. I know you've read that legend about a thousand times. What was the line that the engineer said when he found the crossbow? Ông Ngoại mentioned it in his speech."

"Oh yeah, right." Duy squeezed his eyes shut in concentration. "His favorite quote. It's written all over his journal."

"Yes! Yes! What was it!"

"'Look at all this death. All this destruction. And for what?'" started Duy.

Freddie joined him as they said the last sentence together. "'They shall never be together again.'"

Duy shook his head. "So what?"

"They shall never be together again," Freddie repeated with a grin.

She had it. It was the rare feeling she got when she turned in a test and she knew she'd aced it, except times a million. Ever since Freddie had arrived in Vietnam, she hadn't been confident about anything. But now, she had never been more confident than she was in her current theory. She knew exactly where the turtle's claw was. Her grandfather was right. The answers were in the fairy tale all along.

She grabbed Duy by the shoulders, ignoring his wincing. "I'm going after the crossbow."

"Weren't you listening to anything they said? The crossbow doesn't work—"

"Listen to me," said Freddie. She made sure her tone was sharp. This wasn't Freddie goofing around with humor to lighten a tense situation. No more jokes. No more quips. *They shall never be together again. Don't you get it? Cao Lỗ wasn't talking about two tragic lovers not being united in heaven or lover's eternity or whatever. He was talking about the crossbow and the turtle claw. The tumbler! Don't you see? Cao Lỗ removed the turtle's claw from the crossbow—separating them so that the crossbow could never be used again!"

Duy rubbed his forehead. "Okay now *my* brain hurts. So if the turtle claw isn't with the crossbow . . . where is it?"

Freddie smirked. "You want me to tell you?"

"You're loving this aren't you?"

"Very much so," she said, rubbing her hands. "Spoiler alert. I've been carrying the claw around this whole time." She raised her hand. The bracelet dangled from her wrist. She unhooked the clasp and let the gold chain slither out one end and coil on the ground, leaving the stone in her palm.

The curved dark stone wasn't actually a stone at all.

It was a turtle's claw.

"And Duy, you're gonna love the next part of my plan," said Freddie. She knew she had to get Liên's attention first. And in a way that wouldn't notify Con Hổ or the guards. Freddie cupped her hands around her mouth and gave the best old man bird call she could muster. "*Quac-quac, quac-quac-quac!*"

It did the trick. Liên's brows furrowed and then a smile crept on her. If Con Hổ heard Freddie's bird call, he didn't seem to care. He continued to flip his knife, focused on Ông Ngoại. Liên scanned for Freddie until she found her. Their eyes met. As Freddie's eyes welled with tears, she spotted that Liên's eyes were glistening as well. They'd have plenty time to make up later. Because that was the thing with Viet cousins—you could never stay mad at them forever. They would always come around. Freddie knew that. Liên knew that.

"Now what?" whispered Duy.

"When Liên takes down Con Hổ, I'm going for it."

Duy nearly choked. "Liên? Take down Con Hổ?! I'm going to pretend I didn't hear that."

"I trust her, Duy. She can do this." Freddie turned back to her cousin and pointed to her neck.

Liên's hand reached up and touched the frayed fringes of her checkered scarf. She looked positively baffled.

Freddie nodded. The cousins spoke with their eyes. Suddenly Liên knew what Freddie was asking for, and she nodded in return. Liên slowly unraveled the scarf from her neck and wrapped both ends around her wrists.

Now they were on the same page.

CHAPTER 21

Freddie held her breath. Liên had received her message. Now it was all up to her.

Liên sprung on her heels. Con Hổ was right on her—just as Freddie knew he would be. As he gripped his knife, Liên spun around and wrapped the scarf around his arm. She was quick. It was like watching a spider spin a web to trap a fly. Con Hổ found his arm tangled up in the scarf, and Liên tugged with all her might. Being taken by surprise combined with Liên's technique was enough for Con Hổ to stagger and drop his knife.

Everyone was stunned. But Freddie snapped out of her stupor first and bolted for the table. In one smooth, seamless motion, she grabbed the crossbow in one hand

and held the claw in the other. She slammed the claw into the open groove of the crossbow. A satisfying click echoed off the cave walls.

By this time, Con Hổ had overtaken Liên, keeping his beefy arm around her collar. He wouldn't make the same mistake again.

"Freddie?" Ông Ngoại tried to stand, but Con Hổ forced him back into his seat.

Freddie trained the crossbow at Con Hổ. Suddenly, a single arrow materialized—glittered in the chamber, the turtle claw pulling the phantom string taut. The arrow was almost translucent, as if it were made of light.

"Let her go, Con Hổ," she said.

"You're very good at finding things." Nhất stepped out from the shadows. Behind him, all the guards rushed to take their positions. Some stood their ground by Nhất on both sides. Some took to the second and third levels of the caves. Most of them carried rifles.

Freddie felt a warmth radiating from the crossbow that seemed to flow over her, causing the tips of her toes and fingers to prickle—a calm sort of serenity, despite the fact that she was surrounded by armed guards. She knew she was in control. "Drop your weapons."

"I'm afraid I can't have them do that, con." Nhất

raised his hand, signaling to his crew. A cacophony of clicks. They were going to fire.

Use my power, a familiar baritone voice echoed in Freddie's head. The golden turtle. *You have the power to punish those who dare try to harm you and the ones you love. Do it. Do it now.*

For a moment, time stood still as Freddie considered the divine power in her hands. No mortal should've been able to feel this. It felt good. Tempting. And the turtle-god was right: She could use this power to punish those who have harmed her family. She could take revenge on Nhất—not just for what he'd done to her and to Liên and to Ông Ngoại, but for what he'd done to Duy too. After all, was there ever a nobler thing a person could do? There was a part of Freddie that could understand why a king would never want to let this power go.

And now it was hers. All hers.

But . . . there was another part of Freddie that knew this wasn't the way. She knew how the old legend had ended. Did she really want history to repeat itself? Was this truly her destiny?

No, she thought. *There must be another way.*

Then you must do what you feel is right, the turtle

said. *You control the crossbow. You control the arrows. You control your destiny . . .*

With that, the turtle's voice had gone silent, and Freddie's attention snapped back to reality.

"Drop the crossbow, con," Nhất said. "You don't have the will to do what needs to be done."

Nhất started to lower his hand but Freddie pulled the trigger first.

A loud twang rang out.

As the golden arrow of light flew through the air, filling the cave with a yellow, electric light, it split itself, multiplying again and again and again. The single arrow splintered into hundreds, each one zipping around the enormous cavern like an angry swarm of bees and finding their targets. The golden glow from all the arrows lit up the room like the sky on the Fourth of July.

"No," said Freddie, feeling a bead of sweat drip down her forehead. She focused her fear—channeling it into the arrows. "I'm going to do it my way."

The arrows obeyed her will, freezing in place, suspended in mid-air. The tips of the arrowheads only inches from the guards. Some hovered over their chests, some hovered right between their wide, terror-filled eyes, their mouths agape in horror. And one by one, Freddie could hear the sound of their guns clattering to the ground. The guards, every single one of them, raised their hands in surrender.

Ông Ngoại, Liên, and Duy watched the scene wide eyed.

"Me and my family are all walking out of here. Right now. Ông Ngoại, Liên, let's get out of . . ."

But before she could finish, something flashed past her. Then a searing pain shot through her wrist. Blood dripped, blotting at her feet. She dropped the crossbow, clutching her bleeding hand. The arrows frizzled into nothingness.

Behind her, Con Hổ's knife stuck into the sand.

Nhất grinned. "Mercy is weakness. You shouldn't have hesitated." He strolled to the fallen crossbow and crouched down . . .

But Duy was quicker. He scooped up the crossbow in a flash. Another golden arrow appeared in the chamber. The turtle's claw was in place, ready to fire at Duy's command.

"Oh, by all means, after you, son." Nhất stopped in his tracks, bowing. "Pull the trigger. For once in your life, prove me wrong."

"Leave him alone," snarled Freddie, clutching her

bleeding hand. She knew that the turtle's voice was now ringing in Duy's ears, urging him to use the crossbow's power.

"Americans are always so quick to be the hero, to be brave," spat Nhất, whipping back to face her. "Are you a hero, con? You think you're brave?"

Freddie had about ten good retorts ready, but she bit her tongue. She wouldn't give him the satisfaction.

"No? I didn't think so." Nhất paced, his hands behind his back. Duy kept the crossbow trained on his father. "We're Pháns. Descendants of An Dương Vương himself. Our family was destined for greatness until it was stripped from us. Our story is not yet complete." He stretched his arms wide, soaking in the stream of moonlight. Faint misty rain sprinkled on his face. "What will happen next? That's a matter of destiny as well."

Duy's eyes shone as they filled with tears. "This isn't you, Ba. This isn't who you really are. The crossbow's power is a curse. It always has been. We're not in control! We've never been in control."

"So then use it!" snapped Nhất, his eyes ablaze. "You and I both share the same burden. Father and son. Go on then." He stepped right up to Duy. The tip of the golden arrow almost touched his chest. Then he gently pushed the crossbow so that it aimed toward Con Hổ.

"I . . . I don't . . . want to." The words tumbled out of Duy's mouth, but his eyes told a different truth. Through his tears, Duy's pupils flashed, a glint of gold flickering in them. His hands trembled. His finger twitched on the crossbow's trigger.

"The crossbow is ours. It belongs to us, to our family. Its power was meant to be wielded. Use it." The veins in Nhất's neck bulged. He snarled with such fury and his jaw muscles twitched that Freddie thought he might shatter his own teeth. "You're weak."

Freddie couldn't stand being silent any longer. "No he isn't. Being compassionate and trusting aren't weaknesses."

"Do it. Pull the trigger!"

Beads of sweat dotted Duy's forehead. His short breaths came in pulsating spurts. He looked pale. "I want to use it. I want this power."

"Duy, it isn't you," Freddie cautioned. "You know it isn't."

"But . . . it could solve everything."

Freddie refused to let up. "You're a fighter, Duy."

"I can't hold out much longer, Freddie." His whispers were rushed. The golden light in his eyes burned so intensely, his pupils could no longer be seen. "Help me."

"You don't need me!" Freddie shouted. She knew that the turtle was speaking to Duy now—his words like silk, convincing Duy to embrace the power of the claw. "You can stop this all on your own. It *has* to be you."

"I'm . . . not strong . . . like you."

"No." Freddie placed a hand on his trembling forearm with the same concern and gentleness she had when she placed her hand on his head during his nightmare. "You're stronger."

Duy slowly lowered the crossbow and grunted, struggling to fight something inside himself. The gold glint radiating from his pupils flickered.

Then, in one motion Duy snapped the crossbow upright again, taking aim. He was going to do it. He was going to pull the trigger and there was nothing more Freddie could do to stop him.

"Duy, no!" Freddie shouted, bracing herself for the worst.

But the arrows never came.

Instead of firing, Duy ripped the turtle claw from its chamber, then raised it high in the air.

"It's yours!" His voice was strained—ragged and raw.

"It belongs to you. It should have been returned a long time ago."

His hand shook violently as a brilliant, blinding light burst from the claw seeping through the cracks of his fist. It was as if the sun was captured in a colander. Freddie had to use her arm to cover her eyes, the light was so intense.

Duy grit his teeth, his arm vibrating.

Then the light was gone.

Duy brought is hand down and opened his fist. The claw had vanished.

Nhất instantly fell to his knees. He raised a trembling hand to his face. His dilated eyes darted around the room as if taking everything in for the first time.

"Are you alright, Ba?" Duy said.

Nhất's jaw swung open. "I . . . I feel like . . . you've pulled me from a nightmare."

Duy exhaled, sitting down hard, all his energy sapped from him. The now powerless crossbow clattered to the ground. "I don't think we have to worry about night-mares anymore, Ba." They sat across from each other, but not necessary together.

Ông Ngoại and Liên rushed over to either side of Freddie, both wrapping their arms around her in a tight hug. Ông Ngoại sniffed her cheek. Liên nodded in Duy's direction.

Freddie waved to him. A weak smile spread across Duy's face. The golden light that once burned in his eyes had completely vanished.

The legend of Nỏ Định Mệnh was over.

CHAPTER 22

"I can't believe you're leaving tomorrow," said Liên, plopping down on the bed. "I feel like you just got here."

"Really? It feels like I spent three lifetimes here already," joked Freddie. "But in a good way!" She finished typing out her last text and hit send before tucking her phone away.

"How's Duy doing?" asked Liên, winking.

"About as good as you'd expect someone who just broke a couple-thousand-year-old curse to be," said Freddie. "He'll figure it out. He's tough."

"Duy turned out to be pretty okay in the end." Liên smiled.

It had been a few days since they returned from Đà Nẵng. Things had only just started to calm down. It seemed like there was an endless loop of investigators coming in and out of the house. No one was quite sure what to tell them. Who would believe what really transpired under the mountains?

"We haven't really had a chance to talk about what happened," Freddie said. "It feels like a dream . . . or a nightmare." Freddie looked at her bandaged hand. "Can I tell you something?"

"Yeah."

"When you got taken away, that was the most scared I've ever been." Freddie exhaled, hoping it would steady the tremble in her voice. "Ever since I've been back, I feel like I don't even know who I am or what I should be doing. Like I'm two pieces that don't fit together or something. And I couldn't have done this alone. I couldn't have done this without you."

Liên pushed her new glasses up the bridge of her nose. "Freddie, I never should have said all that stuff to you back in the jungle. I'm sorry. It was totally cruel, and I didn't mean any of it. You know that, right?"

"Yeah," said Freddie, swallowing the lump in her throat. "And I'm sorry for not listening to you. I thought

I was protecting you by taking it all on myself and calling all the shots, and that wasn't cool."

"You're like, one of the coolest people I know," Liên said. "You always have been. You nailed Con Hổ right in his stupid face with nothing but durian. You fought off an angry boar to get us that cave. You faced a golden turtle-god. You discovered the secret of the crossbow and used it to save us all. And . . . you believed in me."

"Technically, you were the one who took down Con Hổ with those sweet scarf moves," said Freddie. "Can you teach me sometime?"

Liên raised her fists, shadow boxing. "Only if you promise to come back across the Atlantic every so often to keep up on your lessons."

"Does that mean we're okay?" The tears flowed down her cheeks, and Freddie didn't fight them.

"We're cousins. Viet cousins. That's like the strongest bond in the universe."

Freddie pulled Liên in for a hug. A relief washed over her—a very rare relief that came with sharing a confused piece of yourself with your best friend.

There was a knock at the door. Mom poked her head in. "Come on, gals, everyone is downstairs waiting."

As Freddie and Liên came down the stairs to the restaurant portion of the house, they were met with a barrage of hugs and cheek-kisses from the aunts and uncles. Ever since they came home, it seemed like someone was hugging them or kissing their cheeks anytime they entered a room.

The spread was enormous as it always was. The uncles poured tall glasses of beer for each other. Of course, everyone had bowls of the family's bún cá, a fish broth noodle soup teeming with leafy green vegetables. Miniature dishes of bánh bèo, mini rice flour pancakes sprinkled with crispy pork skin and dried shrimp, were stacked high.

Everyone was talking over one another in excited Vietnamese. It was so frantic and chaotic, Freddie couldn't parse out what exactly was being said. But something had changed since Freddie first stepped foot in her old home: she didn't feel the hot, queasy embarrassment and shame creep up on her. She watched as her family laughed hard, ate heartily, and shouted over one another other in a way that only families did. She may not have understood every single thing being said, but Freddie understood what a hug meant and what a kiss meant, and that was enough.

Freddie contented herself with a cup of chè ba màu, a pudding made of coconut, mung beans, green jelly, and a layer of sweet red beans. She grabbed a second helping, stepped outside, and crossed the courtyard to her grandfather's room.

Freddie found Ông Ngoại sitting at the edge of his bed gazing at the once-empty glass case. Inside was Nỏ Định Mệnh, the crossbow—without the turtle claw. When his eyes met Freddie's, he waved her over. Palm down in the Vietnamese tradition, of course. She joined him at the edge of the bed, and he put his arm around her. She handed him the extra cup of chè. For a long time, they ate their desserts in silence.

"You like the souvenir I brought back for you?" Freddie joked.

"I never thought I'd see the day when the crossbow would be in that case." Ông Ngoại's eyes twinkled in admiration. "When I finally concluded that Nỏ Định Mệnh was beneath The Marble Mountains . . . everything in that moment changed for me. It was like something snapped me awake. I spent my entire life searching for the crossbow, and all it took was one revelation to realize that it wasn't meant to be discovered. That possessing a weapon of that magnitude was far beyond me. I knew that I couldn't let anyone discover its true location. But you found it. In a little under a week."

"Just lucky, I guess."

Ông Ngoại's eyebrow arched. "Lucky? Freddie. It wasn't luck. It's never been luck with you, con."

Freddie thought for a moment. "Oh yeah? Then what about the turtle claw? I only found it and wore it because of your ceremony. What if I'd picked out another bracelet? Or what if I hadn't worn jewelry at all?"

"Some might call that"—Ông Ngoại winked—"destiny."

Freddie rested her head on her grandfather's shoulder. "Yeah, right. Did you know that I actually saw the golden turtle? He came to me in, like, a vision."

"Wow. Now *that's* lucky."

"You know what he said to me? He said, 'You have the gift.'" Freddie's cheeks went hot, and she shook her head. "For a second, I thought that maybe he was telling me I was special. That I had something in me that made me special. But he wasn't talking about me at all. The gift he was talking about was his own claw—the claw he'd gifted to the king."

Ông Ngoại put his hand on top of hers. "Or maybe you possess something more than a gift. You saved me.

You saved your cousin. And from what I understand, you saved that young man, didn't you?"

"Liên took down Con Hổ all by herself."

Right on cue, there was a yelp that directed their attention to the courtyard where the rest of the family had gathered. Liên was in the middle of giving a Bà Trà demonstration, having just flipped over Bác Thanh to the delight of the brothers and sisters. Bác Hoa clapped the loudest, pulling her daughter into a tight squeeze and sniffing her on the cheek. Liên beamed, her hands planted firmly on her hips.

"And Duy resisted the crossbow's power," continued Freddie, matter-of-factly. "I didn't do much."

"You know, in my line of work, I've read about and researched all different kinds of heroes. Some are brave. Some are selfless. Some were destined for greatness, born with their natural gifts." Ông Ngoại squeezed Freddie's hand. "But you know what the most revered heroes do?"

Freddie shook her head. She didn't have a clue.

"The heroes that stand the test of time are the ones who have been able to shift their perspective—to see clearly," he said. "They have an uncanny ability to see their loved ones for who they truly are and what they are capable of."

Freddie nodded. She wasn't entirely sure she understood, but she couldn't ignore the little hairs on her arms rising.

He sniffed the top of her head. That comforting sniff she was worried she'd never feel again. "Freddie, you saw it in Liên. You saw it in Duy. Now it's time for you to see yourself for who *you* really are. Can you see it? Can you see that you're enough?"

Freddie sat for a moment. For the first time since being back in Vietnam, she did. She was enough.

"Come with me, con." Ông Ngoại stood up and opened the door to the courtyard. "Let's spend your last night together with our family."

Freddie followed Ông Ngoại out to the courtyard but stopped under the mangosteen tree.

She stood on her tiptoes, plucking a ripe mangosteen. Mangosteen was a strange fruit. A fruit that required balance or it wouldn't survive. Mangosteen trees were stubborn, but if they were given exactly what they needed, they'd thrive.

Just like her.

Freddie smiled and took a bite.

GLOSSARY

TK

ACKNOWLEDGMENTS

The second book isn't easier and it took a whole lot of generous, dedicated folks to help make it a reality.

My agent Alyssa Jennette. Another one in the books (get it?). Thank you for your unwavering support and enthusiasm for everything I shove at you. Look at us go!

My editor, Orlando Dos Reis. In 2018, you predicted that we'd work on a book together someday. It wasn't in the cards then, but I'll never forget the call I received from you two years later saying that it was time to finally fulfill your prophecy. Thank you for flooding my inbox with brilliant notes, not letting up until we cracked a puzzle, and of course, the endless supply of *The Mummy* memes and *Avatar: The Last Airbender* gifs. If it wasn't for you, I don't know if I would have even gotten around to booking those plane tickets to a country I knew only from other people's anecdotes and photographs. We built this story together plank by plank. Let's do it again sometime!

Thank you to all my cousins—all one thousand of you. This is a story about the unrivaled bond between Viet cousins and I'd be remiss if I didn't call out one cousin in particular. To Amy, my personal shopper, my travel agent, my translator, and my best pal. When I finally gave in and admitted I couldn't write this book without going to Vietnam, I knew there was only one person who would agree to go with me on a last-minute whim. I couldn't have done it without your meticulous itinerary planning and the generous nature that has always come naturally to you. Thanks for letting me borrow my niece's name and for always being up for an adventure. When is our next trip?

Wylie and KJ: Thank you for letting me spend an entire afternoon at your house while you helped me crack that climatic third act set piece. Put it on my tab.

To production editor Janell Harris and copyeditor Rye White, who combed through this manuscript like a . . . fine . . . comb (see? This is why I need you). You have an incredible superpower that I covet. Thank you for letting me borrow your godlike abilities for a little while.

To Yuta Onoda. Thank you for sharing your stunning artwork for my little book, and thanks to designer Chris Stengel for bringing it all together.

To everyone on the Scholastic team who had a hand in helping this beast of a story come to fruition. You put yourselves in this manuscript, and for that, I'll always be grateful.

Thank you to the booksellers and librarians who have taken a chance on this book. You're doing the good work and I'll continue to fight the good fight right alongside you.

To Jes Vũ for always responding to a "help me!" text at any given hour and being a champion for all things Viet. Thank you to the Vietnamese authors, screenwriters, book bloggers, and entertainers who have not only consistently shown up and supported me, but for all Viets in the arts. You're all my cousins now.

My gals Trixie and Margot: Thank you for the big hugs, big kisses, and forgiving me for all the nights I had to "go to the back office." It was because of our read-aloud Vietnamese legends marathons that I found the inspiration to write this book. My favorite little readers. As always, I write these stories for you.

And most of all, thank you to my wife Beth. I never would have had the guts to take a chance on myself to write books without your insistence. Thank you for your love and being my rock after all these years. I'm so lucky to have married a ravenous bibliophile who endures my long-winded rambles whenever I'm trying to solve a story problem. An extra bit of gratitude for the coverage when I had to panic-book a yurt for a weekend to make deadlines. I love you.

And finally, to everyone who decided to spend their time reading my words. I'm your biggest fan.

About the Author

Brandon Hoàng is the author of *The Crossbow of Destiny* and the young adult novel *Gloria Buenrostro Is Not My Girlfriend*. Born and raised in the Pacific Northwest, Brandon grew up coveting The Baby-Sitters Club books and slurping noodles. Before he was a writer, Brandon was an animation executive. Now a screenwriter by day and novelist by night, he currently resides in Los Angeles with his wife and two daughters.